### *Marcus watched her.*

It was all he was allowed to do. Watch. As she danced with one cowboy after another. He wanted to grab her and throw her over his shoulder and carry her out of there bodily. But he could never do any such thing. She was his princess and he lived to serve her. And that meant, when it came right down to his will versus hers, she held all the cards.

No matter that there was going to be trouble as the evening wore on and the liquor kept flowing. He would probably have to hurt someone. He didn't particularly look forward to that.

But then again, the more cowboys she danced with and the more he was forced to stand there and watch them put their common hands on her person, the more he felt heat building in his chest and behind his eyes, the more hurting someone began to seem like a good and necessary thing.

D1055121

Dear Reader,

For eight years, Rhiannon Bravo-Calabretti, Princess of Montedoro, has tried to forget her first love, a commoner with a tragic childhood who is now a dedicated Montedoran soldier, Captain Marcus Desmarais. Though Rhia truly loved him, Marcus believed himself beneath her and insisted they end their secret love affair. He walked away and did not look back.

Some of you may remember Marcus. In last December's *The Rancher's Christmas Princess,* he was Belle Bravo-Calabretti's ever-present, ever-watchful bodyguard.

Now Marcus has a new assignment. He's to provide security to the one woman he can never forget: Rhia. The Bravo-Calabretti princes are traveling to Montana for a wedding. Belle, Rhia's sister, is marrying the rancher who won her heart last Christmas. The trip won't be a long one. Both Rhia and Marcus tell themselves that all they have to do is endure each other's presence for a few days and then they can go their separate ways once again.

Fate, however, has other plans for these two. And when the wedding party is over, Marcus and Rhia will find it harder than ever to turn and walk away from the love they've spent much too long trying to deny.

Happy reading,

Christine

# HER HIGHNESS AND THE BODYGUARD

## *CHRISTINE RIMMER*

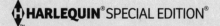
HARLEQUIN® SPECIAL EDITION®

If you purchased this book without a cover you should be aware
that this book is stolen property. It was reported as "unsold and
destroyed" to the publisher, and neither the author nor the
publisher has received any payment for this "stripped book."

Recycling programs
for this product may
not exist in your area.

ISBN-13: 978-0-373-65733-9

HER HIGHNESS AND THE BODYGUARD

Copyright © 2013 by Christine Rimmer

All rights reserved. Except for use in any review, the reproduction
or utilization of this work in whole or in part in any form by any
electronic, mechanical or other means, now known or hereafter
invented, including xerography, photocopying and recording, or in
any information storage or retrieval system, is forbidden without
the written permission of the publisher, Harlequin Enterprises Limited,
225 Duncan Mill Road, Don Mills, Ontario M3B 3K9, Canada.

This is a work of fiction. Names, characters, places and incidents are
either the product of the author's imagination or are used fictitiously, and
any resemblance to actual persons, living or dead, business establishments,
events or locales is entirely coincidental.

This edition published by arrangement with Harlequin Books S.A.

For questions and comments about the quality of this book, please contact us
at CustomerService@Harlequin.com.

® and TM are trademarks of Harlequin Enterprises Limited or its corporate
affiliates. Trademarks indicated with ® are registered in the United States Patent
and Trademark Office, the Canadian Trade Marks Office and in other countries.

**Printed in U.S.A.**

# Books by Christine Rimmer

---

## CHRISTINE RIMMER

came to her profession the long way around. Before settling down to write about the magic of romance, she'd been everything from an actress to a salesclerk to a waitress. Now that she's finally found work that suits her perfectly, she insists she never had a problem keeping a job—she was merely gaining "life experience" for her future as a novelist. Christine is grateful not only for the joy she finds in writing, but for what waits when the day's work is through: a man she loves who loves her right back, and the privilege of watching their children grow and change day to day. She lives with her family in Oregon. Visit Christine at www.christinerimmer.com.

For my parents,
Tom and Auralee Smith,
who shared sixty-five amazing years together
and taught me what true love can do.

## Chapter One

How could this have happened?

Rhiannon Bravo-Calabretti, princess of Montedoro, could not believe it. Honestly. What were the odds?

One in ten, maybe? One in twenty? She supposed that it could have just been the luck of the draw. After all, her country was a small one and there were only so many rigorously trained bodyguards to be assigned to the members of the princely family.

However, when you added in the fact that Marcus Desmarais wanted nothing to do with her ever again, reasonable odds became pretty much no-way-no-how. Because he would have said no.

So why hadn't he?

A moment later, she realized she knew why: because if he refused the assignment, his superiors might ask questions. Suspicion and curiosity could be roused and he wouldn't have wanted that.

*Stop.*

Rhia sat very still in the old wooden pew with her hands folded tightly in her lap.

What did it matter, why or how this had happened? The point was it *had* happened.

Enough. Done. She was simply not going to think about it—about *him*—anymore.

The wedding Mass was in English and the priest was concluding the homily drawn from scripture on the subject of Christian marriage. Rhia stared resolutely forward, trying to focus on the words. On the spare beauty of this little Catholic church in the small town of Elk Creek, Montana, where her sister was getting married.

The white-frame Church of the Immaculate Conception was simple and charming, as white inside as out. It smelled of candle wax and lemon furniture polish, with a faint echo of damp outerwear and old incense. The worn pews were of oak and all of them were full. Those who hadn't found seats stood at the back and along the sides.

*He* would be standing. In back somewhere by the doors, silent. And unobtrusive. Just like the other security people. Her shoulders ached from the tension, from the certainty that he was watching her, those eerily level, oh-so-serious, almost-green eyes staring twin holes into the back of her head.

*It doesn't matter. Forget about it, about him.*

What mattered was Belle.

Sweet, dignified, big-hearted Belle, all in white and positively radiant, standing at the plain altar before the communion rail with a tall, rugged American rancher named Preston McCade. It was a double ceremony. Belle's longtime companion, Lady Charlotte of the notorious Mornay branch of the family, was also getting married—to Preston McCade's father, a handsome old charmer named Silas.

"All rise," said the priest.

Rhia stood up with everyone else. The priest made a little speech about the rite of marriage and proceeded to question both the brides and the grooms about their intentions—their freedom of choice and faithfulness, their willingness to accept God's great gift of children.

And Rhia couldn't help it. Her mind relentlessly circled back to the subject of Marcus.

It just made no sense, she kept thinking. He wanted nothing to do with her. He wouldn't have chosen this.

So then, who *had* made the choice? Did someone else know about what had once happened between them, about those magical, unforgettable weeks so far in the past? Rhia had told one person. Only one. And that person was someone she trusted absolutely to say nothing. Marcus would have told no one. Which meant that no one else could possibly know.

Could they? A cold shiver slid down her spine. Was that what had happened here? Somehow, someone else did know and had decided to throw them together like this for some completely incomprehensible reason?

No. That made no sense. The very idea was ridiculous. What possible benefit could there be to anyone in forcing proximity upon them?

And besides, who else could know? It had been so long ago—eight years. Which was three years before her brother Alex had been kidnapped in Afghanistan, back when her family wasn't so terribly security conscious.

At the time, Rhia had been a freshman at UCLA. Once she was settled in her dorm and going to classes, she'd had no one watching over her. She'd enjoyed being just another student, like all the other students. Her private life at that time had been simply that: private. After all, she was sixth in line to the throne, with four brothers and Belle ahead of her. Plus, Rhia had always been a well-behaved sort of person. Between her good-girl reputation and the extreme unlikelihood that she would ever end up on Montedoro's throne, she'd been of little interest to the scandal sheets.

Which was why she still believed that no one else knew.

At the altar, the ceremony had progressed to the exchange of vows. Rhia stood a little straighter and tried to concentrate on the beautiful, familiar words.

"I, Preston, take you, Arabella, for my lawful wife, to have and to hold, from this day forward…"

Rhia knew she was making too much of this. She should just…let it go. Let it be. Marcus wasn't going to bother her. He was all about duty and keeping to his "place," just as he'd always been. He'd hardly spoken three words to her since yesterday, when they boarded the family jet at Nice and she learned he would provide her security during this trip.

Why he'd been assigned to her didn't matter. He was there to protect her, period. And she only had to get through this one day and the evening. Tomorrow, she would fly home again.

And be free of him.

Forever.

Rhia released a slow sigh. Yes. It would be all right. She smiled a little, watching her beautiful sister. Belle was saying her vows now, her eyes only for her groom, her fine-boned face seeming to glow from within. "I, Arabella, take you, Preston…"

In the front pew, Benjamin, Preston's toddler, let out a happy trill of laughter and called, "Belle, Dada, Shar-Shar, Pawpaw!" The guests laughed, too, as Belle, her groom, Charlotte and *her* groom paused to turn and wave at the little one, who sat on the lap of a sturdy-looking older lady.

A moment later, Belle began her vows all over again.

Yes. Truly. It was only for one more day, Rhia reminded herself, her heavy mood lightened by the laughter of the little boy.

She could bear anything for a single day—a day that was already halfway through. It had been a shock, that was all. And now she was past it.

She would simply ignore him. How hard could that be?

Really hard.

Harder by the hour, by the minute. By the second, for heaven's sake.

After the ceremony, the brides, the grooms and Belle and Rhia's parents, Her Sovereign Highness Adrienne and His Serene Highness Evan, held a receiving line in the vestibule. Rhia got to hug Belle and Charlotte and wish them all the love and happiness in the world, and to congratulate the two grooms.

Then there were pictures. Rhia had to stay for those. Belle and Charlotte had chosen to forgo attendants and there were no groomsmen, but Belle wanted her family— her parents and sisters and brothers—in the photographs. So that took more than an hour. Outside the sun hovered just above the craggy, snowcapped mountaintops and the temperature was dropping.

The whole time they lingered at the church, Marcus lurked just beyond Rhia's line of sight. He had a knack for staying out of the way and yet, somehow, always remaining nearby, for keeping her constantly in his view. His expression, whenever she made the mistake of sliding a nervous glance in his direction, was as still and unreadable as a bottomless pool in some secret, hidden place.

She did try to ignore him, something so easily done with any other man. She tried so very hard not to turn her head his way, not to look at him.

But it was no good. He seemed to be everywhere—and nowhere—at once. And she needed so strongly to pick him out of the crowd, to pin him in space, to know for certain where, exactly, he was.

The photographer was posing a shot of Belle and Charlotte holding the beaming Benjamin between them, when Silas and Preston McCade came toward her. At first, Rhia thought the two men intended to speak with her. But then, with matching nods and smiles and a couple of murmured greetings in her direction, they moved on by.

She turned to watch them step right up to Marcus.

Marcus nodded at father and son. "Gentlemen." His voice so deep and solemn and contained. "Congratulations."

Silas laughed and held out his hand. "Good to see you, Marcus. Place ain't the same without you."

Marcus took the older man's offered hand and spoke again, quietly enough that Rhia couldn't make out the words. Silas and Preston both chuckled.

And Rhia was left turning, lurching away. Stunned. Stricken, that Marcus could be almost friendly with the McCade men while behaving like a bleak and watchful stranger around her. Yes, she already knew that he'd been assigned to Belle when Belle came to America to nurse her terminally ill friend, Anne, who was Benjamin's mother. But that he'd remained with Belle when Belle brought Benjamin to Montana? She'd had no idea, not until just now when the McCade men had greeted him.

Dear God, Rhia hated all the secrecy. All the lies. She was not in any way ashamed of having loved Marcus. She didn't want to keep the secrets and she didn't want to tell the lies. Marcus wanted all that. And all those years ago, she'd foolishly promised him that they would do it his way.

Thus, she had only become aware that Marcus had previously been assigned to Belle when she flew to North Carolina for Anne's funeral. She'd seen him there, guarding Belle, and been as hollowed-out and desolate at the sight of him as she was right now.

Except that now was worse because today he was watching *her* and there was no escaping him.

Rhia slipped through the wide-open oak doors to the vestibule, driven to get away from him, though she knew it was hopeless. He would only have to follow her.

In the vestibule, her sister Alice appeared at her side, all dimples and laughing eyes, her brown hair a wild mass of loose curls to her shoulders. She wrapped an arm around Rhia and whispered, "How are you managing?"

"Don't ask."

Alice chuckled. "Oops. Sorry. I already did."

Rhia loved, admired and trusted all four of her sisters. But with Alice, the bond went even deeper. They were not only siblings, they were best friends. They told each other everything. And they had sworn from childhood to protect and respect each others' confidences. Rhia needed one person in her life to whom she could say anything. Alice was that person. And Rhia told her everything. Alice was the one who knew about Marcus.

Marcus stepped through the open doors into the vestibule. Spotting her instantly, he slid back into the shadows along the wall, where he was out of the way yet could keep her in sight.

"This is ridiculous," Rhia muttered out of the side of her mouth. "I can't get away from him and it's driving me insane. I'm pathetic. How can I possibly care this much?"

Alice moved in front of Rhia, facing her, blocking Marcus's view of her. Now they could talk without the unpleasant possibility that Marcus would overhear them or read their words from their lips.

"If it's so unbearable," Alice suggested low, "talk to Alex. Tell him you want someone else." Their brother Alexander had created the elite fighting force called the Covert Command Unit, or CCU, in which Marcus served. Right now, Alex was back in the chapel with his wife, Her Royal Highness Liliana of Alagonia, and their three-month-old twins, Melodie and Phillipe.

"If I go to Alex, it will only look bad for Marcus. Plus, it could make Alex wonder if there's something between us."

Alice made a snorty sound—but when she spoke, she did it very quietly. "So what? Deny it."

"It would still reflect negatively on Marcus, you know that."

"Too bad."

Rhia suppressed a sigh and tried to explain in a near whisper, without moving her lips too much. "Haven't we been through this?" She darted glances from side to side. No one seemed to be the least interested in their conversation. "Marcus sees himself as beneath me. He couldn't stand for Alex or anyone else to suspect that there might have been something between us once, that we were…" She let the words trail off. No need to be overly specific. Alice knew, anyway.

Her sister reached out and cupped the side of her face with a soothing hand. "You really must get past all this. You know that, don't you?"

"I'm trying." And she had been trying for eight endless years. During that time she'd had two fiancés. Both good men, each supremely suitable: an internationally known artist from a fine family and a generous duke who worked diligently for a number of worthy charities. Somehow, she hadn't managed to bring herself to marry either of those men. And they had both eventually realized that her heart wasn't in it. The relationships had died. She remained on friendly terms with both of her former fiancés, a fact that made her failure with them all the more wretched. As though both men had realized that there hadn't been enough to what they'd shared in the first place to be bitter or angry over losing it.

"Try harder," Alice suggested with a sigh.

"I know you're right. And I do need to get over it. And I am completely and utterly fed up with myself, with my silly broken heart and my inability to get past something that happened years ago. I want to scream, Allie. I want to scream really, really loud."

"Just hold it together. Just a little while longer." Alice tipped her head in the direction of the open doors to the chapel. "They're finishing up. We'll be leaving for the ranch soon." The reception was to be held in the main house at the McCade family ranch, which was half an hour's drive away. Alice reached out again, still aiming to soothe. She gently stroked Rhia's pinned-up hair. "Just breathe, all right? Stay calm." She lifted her other hand, where she held the keyless ignition remote to the shiny red pickup she'd rented that morning. "You can ride to the ranch with me and the bodyguards can follow us. And after we put in our time there, we'll bust out. You'll have fun and forget all your troubles, I promise you."

Rhia gave her a wary look. "Excuse me. Bust out?"

"It's cowboy country. We'll go wild."

"No, Alice. Seriously."

Allie patted her shoulder. "Trust me. Busting out is the answer. I haven't exactly worked out the logistics yet. But it is going to be good."

Rhia should have nixed the busting out right then and there. It was a bad idea. But she was just upset enough and feeling trapped enough to think that doing something risky and wild wouldn't be half bad. *Anything* to get her mind off the bodyguard she could never quite seem to forget.

She did ride with Alice to the ranch. Marcus, along with Allie's bodyguard, a giant named Altus, followed them in one of the black luxury SUVs that the family had leased for the visit.

Alice kept up a steady stream of cheerful chatter during the ride. She was excited about the electronic key. You carried it on your person and the doors and ignition responded to the touch of your hand. "Amazing, isn't it, the things they come up with these days?"

Rhia tried to appreciate her efforts to brighten the mood. Still, it felt like the drive went on forever. Rhia stared out the windshield at the endless sky that was darkening steadily toward nighttime, at the craggy, shadowed peaks in the distance, and the rolling, open land dotted here and there with patches of leftover snow. She gazed glumly at the patient, hulking shapes of grazing cattle. Alice kept saying how beautiful it all was.

Rhia agreed with her. Montana was stark and beautiful and a little forbidding to a woman raised in a palace on the Mediterranean. It brought to mind the great Western artist, Charles Russell—or at least it did for Rhia, who had studied Russell's work in her History of American Art class when she was at UCLA.

The McCade ranch house was two stories high, made of wood and stone. They'd hired cowboys to act as valets. Allie turned over her electronic key to a tall, lean fellow in a white hat and they went up the wide front steps.

At the door, the two brides and their grooms greeted the guests with hugs and handshakes and happy smiles. There was plenty of good food—what the Americans called home cooking—laid out on the big table in the formal dining room. Guests loaded up plates and sat wherever they could find a chair, in the living room, the family room or the kitchen. Many simply stood in the foyer holding their plates, chatting about the beauty of the simple wedding, about the weather, about the quarter horses the McCade ranch was known for.

Alice, whose life revolved around the fabulous Akhal-Teke horses she bred and trained at home, was on her way out the door to visit the McCade stables the minute she'd finished with the greetings. Before she went, she whispered to Rhia, "Do you have your international driving permit?"

"It's in my clutch bag. The housekeeper took it upstairs with my coat."

"Go up and get it. Just the permit. If you get your bag and coat, you-know-who will guess that something's up."

"What exactly are you planning?"

"I told you. Escape." That was all Alice would say. She turned and went out the door, Altus behind her.

Rhia would have gone, too, but it was cold outside and she cared more than Alice did about preserving her shoes—in this case, a gorgeous pair of blue satin Manolo Blahniks with four-inch heels. And then there was Marcus, who would only follow her out there, which meant that she wouldn't be able to complain further to her sister about the awfulness of the situation, anyway.

So she went upstairs and into the bedroom where all the coats were piled. She found her bag and got her permit and put it in the concealed inner pocket of her silk suit jacket, taking a minute after that to smooth her hair and apply fresh lip gloss so that when she exited the bedroom, Marcus would assume she'd only gone in to freshen up.

He was waiting right there in the upstairs hall when she emerged. Her heart lurched alarmingly at the sight of him. She took care not to make eye contact with him as she turned for the stairs.

Once on the first floor, she proceeded to the dining room, where she piled some food onto a pretty gold-trimmed china plate, grabbed a flute of champagne and mingled with her family and the neighbors and friends that the McCades had known all their lives. She worked hard to keep her spirits up, and she knew she was talking a little too loudly and laughing too much, trying to show both herself and the silent, ever-present bodyguard that she was having a great time and didn't really even notice he was there.

It was exhausting. Her neck ached from keeping her back so straight and holding her chin high. And then there was the tension headache pounding at her temples, battering at the base of her skull. She only wanted to return to Elk Creek, to the motor inn where her family had booked every room, to take a long bath, gulp down some aspirin and climb into bed.

However, if she left now, before Allie returned to rescue her with that big red pickup she'd rented, Marcus would be driving her. She did not want to be trapped alone in a vehicle with Marcus for the ride back.

So she stayed.

"You're scrunching up your forehead," Alice whispered in her ear. She smelled of hay and fresh air.

"I have a splitting headache. Did you just come back inside?"

"I did. Preston and Silas have my complete respect and admiration. The stables are clean and open and well-lighted with excellent turnout into large, grassy pastures. The horses are happy and healthy and beautiful. It's a fine operation. I would love to get a chance to ride while we're here. Too bad we're leaving tomorrow and I failed to bring riding clothes from the Drop On Inn."

"Oh, Allie. You got mud on those fabulous Jimmy Choos."

Alice shrugged. "It was worth it. Did you get the permit?"

"Yes."

"Excellent. I have come up with a plan for you, for *both* of us."

"Uh-oh."

Allie poked her in the ribs. "Don't *uh-oh* me. It's a brilliant plan."

"Like the time you crashed that big BMW motorcycle you borrowed into that poor fruit seller's stand at the open-air market?" The open-air market was a Saturday tradition in Montedoro. Rows of street vendors set up stands and sold fresh produce, meats, baked goods and sundries on the Rue St. Georges.

"That was not a plan." Allie spoke sternly. But her eyes were gleaming. "That was an accident."

"Exactly my point."

Allie leaned closer. "Do you want to get away from him or not?"

Against her better judgment, Rhia slid him a glance. Those eyes that were both cool and smoldering at once gazed back at her. Knowing. Ever watchful. She let out a weary sigh. "You know that I do."

"Then let's go. We'll find some thrilling American bar where they play songs about lost love. We can dance with cowboys and drink tequila and you can forget all your troubles."

"You know he'll only follow us. It *is* his job—and what about *your* bodyguard?" Rhia tipped her head in Altus's direction. Like Marcus, he was close by.

"We'll wait till they both turn away and then we'll duck out."

"But Marcus *never* turns away."

Allie took her hand and dragged her into the dining room. Before the bodyguards could follow, she pressed the truck's electronic key into her palm, closing her fingers around it. "The pickup is right out in front, ready to go. I had the valet bring it up before I came inside."

Rhia opened her palm and saw that the key wasn't the only thing Allie had handed her. "Condoms." There were two of them. "You're not serious."

"Stop looking at your hand. He'll see."

Rhia closed her fist and dropped it to her side. "What could I possibly need condoms for? I'm not going to have sex with a stranger."

"Be prepared, I always say."

"But, Allie, you know me better than that."

"Stop arguing. Get near the front door so you can duck out fast. I'll create a distraction." Her eyes were bright with mischief and excitement.

"Then he'll follow *you*—and you'll lead him to me."

"No, I won't. That's why I gave *you* the key. Because on second thought, I'll stay right here. You're on your own. If you want to get away, do it."

It was a wild and stupid idea and Rhia knew she should simply say no. She wasn't like Allie. Except for that one time with Marcus eight years ago and that other crushing, humiliating event two years after that, Rhia never stepped outside the rules. She inevitably behaved in a manner both dignified and agreeable, as the daughter of an ancient and noble house should. She had a lovely career overseeing acquisitions and restorations at her country's National Museum, a career that was more of an avocation, really, as befitted a princess of Montedoro. She lived a quiet, respectable life in a beautiful little villa with a fine view of the sea.

And look where all that exemplariness had gotten her. Twice engaged to "suitable" men she'd never managed to actually love. Still pretending that she wasn't pining for a man who had made it more than clear that it was long over between them and would forever remain that way.

The man in question was standing in the doorway to the foyer. Watching. Tall, wide-shouldered and beautifully male, with those distant eyes she wanted to drown in and that fine, sculpted mouth she only longed to kiss again....

Fair enough. Maybe Alice had the right idea. Perhaps it *was* time she shook things up a little. "I'll get my coat." She turned for the stairs and the bedroom up there that had been designated as a coat room.

Allie grabbed her hand, yanked her back and whispered in her ear, "You are no good at being bad." Patiently, she explained again, "Remember? If you get your coat, he'll know you're leaving."

"But it's cold out there."

"Believe it or not, the pickup has a heater. And so will the cowboy honky-tonk bar."

"A honky-tonk bar? Where am I supposed to find one of those?"

Allie puffed out her cheeks and crossed her eyes. "Just keep driving until you see one."

"What if I never see one?"

"You will—and you're stalling."

"Am not."

"Are so. Do you want to get away or not?"

"I… If I run away, Marcus could be in trouble for losing track of me."

"That's his problem."

"But I…"

"Rhia. Make up your mind. Are you doing this or not?"

She sucked in a fortifying breath. "I am. Yes. Definitely."

"Then wander over near the front door and wait for me to distract him."

"How will you do that?"

"You'll see."

"Oh, wait. I get it. You don't *know* how you'll do it."

"I will figure out something."

"Allie, I really don't think…"

But her sister was already turning away. And not looking back.

Rhia watched her go and told herself to stop being a coward. She was busting out. It was better to make a move—even a *bad* move—than to go on like this, moping around dear Belle's wedding reception, wishing she could be anywhere but here.

So she slid around the end of a heavy china cabinet where, for a moment or two, Marcus couldn't see as she slipped the car remote and the unnecessary condoms into the pocket of her suit jacket next to her driving permit. Turning, she smoothed her hair and grabbed a bottle of water from the flower-bedecked beverage table. Sipping the water, doing her best to act as though she wasn't going anywhere but a different room, she wandered out into the living room and stood and chatted for a bit with her brother Rule and his wife, Sydney. She cooed over Sydney and Rule's new baby, Ellie, who was the same age as Alex and Lili's twins. She even got a shy kiss from the adorable Trevor, Rule and Sydney's three-year-old.

Eventually, sipping her water and playing it ultracasual, she meandered toward the foyer, pausing to share a few words with anyone who happened to make eye contact with her along the way. In the foyer near the stairs, she chatted up an older couple who were very active in the church where Belle had just gotten married, and then circled around until, at last, she was standing in front of the door.

By then, she was actually having a little fun. Preparing to do something she probably shouldn't wasn't as bad as she'd imagined it might be.

Would Allie be ready to provide the distraction—whatever it was?

And where was Allie, anyway?

No need to ask. Right then, her sister made her move. A sudden shriek had heads whipping toward the door to the living room, where Marcus just happened to be standing—though off to the side a bit. Carrying a plate mounded with food from the buffet table and a tall glass of what appeared to be iced tea, Allie tripped over her slightly muddy Jimmy Choos and lost her balance as Marcus whirled her way and caught her before she ended up facedown on the hardwood floor.

What he didn't catch was the plate of home cooking or the big glass of ice and tea. It all went flying. The food hit him in the face and the tea splashed down the front of his handsome dress uniform.

Rhia didn't stick around to see what happened next. While all eyes were on Alice and the food-and-tea-drenched bodyguard, she opened the front door and slipped through.

## Chapter Two

The big red pickup, shining in the light of the moon, was waiting at the foot of the wide front steps, just as Allie had promised. Breathless and giggling, feeling wild and rather wonderful, Rhia raced down the steps and around to the driver's side.

She was up behind the wheel in a split second. Her hands were steady as she pushed the ignition button. She put the truck in gear and off she went, the tires squealing a little, fishtailing, too, making her feel thrillingly disruptive and undisciplined as she took off down the long driveway that led to the highway.

Halfway to the little town of Elk Creek, driving way too fast, with no one behind her, she threw back her head and laughed out loud. The cab was toasty warm from the pickup's excellent heater and she was on her way somewhere with cowboys and country-western music. She turned on the radio. Wouldn't you know it was set to a country station?

A duet. A man and a woman singing about the hot and dangerous love they once had and how they wanted that again. Rhia turned the sound up good and loud and let the music fill the cab.

She left it up loud. Through that song and the song after that and the ones that followed, too.

When she reached Elk Creek, she slowed down and drove through the town at the speed limit, her eyes scanning the street to either side, looking for that cowboy bar her sister had been so sure she was bound to find.

She saw a steak house called the Bull's Eye and a corner bar called Charlie's Place, but both of them looked way too quiet. Not the kind of establishments where exciting things involving cowboys, tequila shots and line dancing might be going on.

Elk Creek was in her rearview mirror before she even realized she'd driven through and was leaving town. She kept going, the almost-full moon leading her on, her designer shoe pressing the accelerator again. Eventually, Marcus would be coming after her. She needed to be far enough ahead that he wouldn't find her that night.

She should probably turn off the highway, take some other road to throw him off her trail. But if she did that, Lord knew where she'd end up.

Then it occurred to her that she ought to just use the GPS. She pulled off onto the shoulder and fiddled with it until she figured out how to ask it for bars in the vicinity.

What do you know?

Twenty-point-six miles straight ahead. Rowdy's Roadhouse. Music, liquor, pool tables, video poker—and dancing nightly. Just what Allie had promised she'd find if she only went looking.

Humming along to a song about a man who was hard to love, Rhia swung out onto the empty highway again, headed for Rowdy's.

Captain Marcus Desmarais lived to serve his country.

And right now he was doing one craptastic job of it—as the Americans might say.

He drove the black SUV faster than he should have, hardly slowing as he went through Elk Creek, eyes scanning the street, on one side and then the other, looking for a shiny red pickup or a beautiful dark-haired woman dressed in a blue silk suit with a snug jacket and a short, slim skirt that showed off her fine, long legs.

He didn't see either—the woman or the pickup.

That had better mean she was up ahead of him.

She had better not have turned off the main highway. If she'd done that, he might never find her until she was damn good and ready to be found.

But no. He was going to find her and he wasn't allowing himself to think otherwise. He would find her. Or she would come back on her own within the next few hours. He would consider no other possibility. He ground his teeth together, stepped harder on the gas and focused on the road ahead.

An hour. That was how long His Highness Alexander had given him to track her down solo and solve the problem simply, without all the unpleasantness of sounding the alarm. If he couldn't do that, the prince would be calling in reinforcements, which would terrify her family, cast a pall on what should have been a day of joy and celebration and provide fodder for the scandal sheets.

An hour—twenty-five minutes of which were already gone.

Why was she doing this? What could she possibly hope

to prove by endangering herself in this foolish, reckless, pointless way?

The questions didn't even bear asking. He knew very well why. And he knew what she hoped to gain by running: she only wanted to get away from *him*.

He should never have accepted this assignment. He'd known what it meant, that she would hate having him as her protector. Staying well clear of her was essential and had been since those eight unforgettable weeks they'd been together nearly a decade ago. So he should have spoken up, asked to be removed, no matter what the higher-ups made of it. If they'd refused him, at least he would have done what he could.

But he was too proud. And too ambitious. And he didn't want *her* hurt, either—at least, no more than he'd already hurt her. He didn't want anyone wondering why he would refuse such an assignment, didn't want them digging around in the past and maybe, against all odds, learning what had happened so long ago.

So he hadn't spoken up. He hadn't requested a different assignment. He'd left her to turn to her impetuous younger sister to find a way to escape him.

The town vanished behind him. The dark highway lay ahead, growing darker as clouds crept across the face of the moon and obscured the thick wash of bright stars. He pressed the gas harder, adjusted the Bluetooth device in his ear and kept going.

On the radio, a lonely cowboy begged his girl to come over. By then, Rhia had it turned to full volume.

A moment later, Rowdy's Roadhouse appeared up ahead, a wash of lovely, garish light on the dark horizon. "Arriving at your destination in point-two miles," said the GPS. Rhia turned it off.

She slowed as she reached the entrance to the great big parking lot lighted with bright streetlamps on tall poles and chock full of muddy pickups and enormous sport utility vehicles. Rowdy's itself was a gray-shingled square building in the center of the lot, complete with giant neon sign over the door proclaiming it Rowdy's Roadhouse and Motor Inn. The sign had two arrows. One pointed at the door below it, the other straight up—presumably indicating the long, low building at the back of the lot, which had its own neon sign advertising rooms for rent.

Rhia found a space when a big green quad cab pulled out. She parked and patted her pocket with the permit in it. In the USA, bartenders were usually careful to check the age of their patrons.

About then it occurred to her that she had no money. It was going to be difficult to get a beer and a tequila shot without cash or a credit card. But then she shrugged and climbed down from the pickup, anyway. Even without the tequila, she could still dance with a cowboy if one would only cooperate and ask her.

Or maybe she would simply have to be truly bold and do the asking herself.

It was a dirt parking lot. Not good for her satin shoes. Too bad. She'd come this far and she wasn't turning back now, not even at the risk of ruining her favorite Manolos. She locked up the pickup and turned toward the music and neon lights.

Overhead, the sky was a solid sheet of darkness now. Clouds had rolled in and obscured the moon and stars. She wrapped her arms around herself, shivering a little because the night was so cold. There were cowboys leaning against the long rail on the wide front porch of the roadhouse. They watched her come toward them.

One of them let out a long whistle. "Oh, darlin'. Hot and

classy. Just how I like 'em." He was tall and very lean. He grinned at her and she saw he had a wide space between his front teeth.

A red-haired woman in a rhinestone shirt and studded jeans smacked his big hat off his head. "Mind your manners, Bobby Dale, or I won't be responsible for what happens next."

Bobby Dale bent and scooped up his hat. "Be nice, Mona. I was only jokin' around."

Mona made a humphing sound and aimed a wide, friendly smile at Rhia. "Come on in. The music's great and the company is passable."

As it turned out, Mona was the head bartender at Rowdy's. She took Rhia inside and got her a beer and a shot of tequila on the house. At the sight of Rhia's driving permit, which gave her full name but none of her titles, Mona asked, "From Montedoro, huh? You here for Pres McCade's wedding to our princess?"

*Our princess.* Rhia found it rather charming, that already the people of Belle's new community thought of her as "theirs." "I am," she said. "It was a beautiful wedding."

"I knew it would be. We're all mighty fond of Pres, and of Silas. Makes us happy to see two good men find what they've been lookin' for."

The band started up again and a cowboy tapped Rhia on the shoulder. She took a sip of her beer, gave Mona a conspiratorial wink, and off she went to learn a cowboy dance called the two-step.

Twenty minutes later, she'd danced with three more cowboys, each as polite and gentlemanly as the one before. She was having an absolutely perfect time and thinking that maybe she would borrow a phone and make a call or two, see if she could reach Allie to tell her where she was and not to worry and say she would be staying out until midnight or maybe later.

Also, it would be a chance to make sure that no one was too terribly concerned about her having slipped away. She could make it very clear that she was safe and warm and had only had one beer and one tequila shot and would return to the ranch as soon as Rowdy's Roadhouse closed its doors for the night.

Mona was pouring drinks at the other end of the bar. Rowdy's was a busy place that Saturday night and the customers were thirsty. Rhia climbed onto her stool, drained the last of her beer and waited for Mona to glance her way.

She sensed a manly presence behind her. Smiling, she turned to face the cowboy she knew would be standing there, planning to tell him she would be happy to dance with him as soon as she'd made a phone call.

Her heart jumped into her throat and got stuck there, cutting off her air, when she saw that it wasn't a cowboy at all.

It was Marcus.

## Chapter Three

Someone must have come up with a change of clothes for him after his close encounter with all that home cooking on Allie's plate.

He was wearing old jeans and rawhide boots, a dark sweatshirt and a heavy canvas jacket. He smelled of the cold mountain air outside and he looked more dangerous and exciting and wonderful than any of the handsome cowboys she'd danced with so far. His expression, however, was even bleaker than usual.

"Time to go, ma'am." His voice sent the usual infuriating warm shivers cascading through her.

She swallowed her silly heart back down into its proper place and remained on her stool. "No, thank you. I'm having a lovely time and I'm not ready to leave yet."

He frowned rather thunderously and then touched the device in his ear, listening. After a moment, he said, "Yes, sir. All is well, sir. Although Her Highness expresses reluctance to leave."

Rhia groaned. "Is that my brother?"

Marcus granted her a put-upon glance as he spoke again—but not to her. "Yes, sir. I will. Thank you, sir."

The call appeared to have been concluded, so she asked a second time, "My brother?"

He scowled, an expression both dismissive and chock-full of exasperation. "That was His Highness Alexander, yes. Are you ready to go now, ma'am?"

*Ma'am.* He was such a stickler for protocol. You would think he had never seen her naked. She wanted to toss her drink in his face. Unfortunately, it was empty. "No. I am *not* ready to go. If you insist on staying here until I *am* ready, please move away from me." She flung out a hand in the direction of the far wall. "Go over there and lurk in the shadows somewhere. No one will ask me to dance with you standing right next to me, glowering."

He told her again, as if he hadn't already said it twice, "Ma'am, we have to leave."

"No, *we* most certainly do not. Go if you want to. I'm staying."

He stood even straighter—if that was possible. "Ma'am, there's a storm coming."

She answered with excruciating pleasantness. "If you call me *ma'am* one more time, I am going to throw back my head and scream."

He tried again, without expression or vocal inflection—and without saying *ma'am,* either. "There is a snowstorm coming. It could be a bad one. It is imperative that we return to Elk Creek and the safety of the motor lodge."

"What are you talking about? There was no storm predicted."

"I noticed the clouds gathering and I listened to the

weather channel," he explained slowly and patiently, as one would speak to an idiot or a very young child. "There *is* a snowstorm coming. Please take my word for it."

"But it's April. I don't believe you. And even if there is a little snow on the way, look at all these people." She held out her hands, palms out, indicating the large, busy bar and everyone in it. "If the weather is going to be dangerous, why aren't they leaving?"

"It often snows in Montana in April."

"Oh, because *you're* such an expert."

"These people live here. They are accustomed to snowstorms. They have proper outerwear and the right vehicles, which they know how to drive."

"I have the right vehicle. And I can drive it perfectly well. And as to my lack of outerwear, the pickup I drove here has a heater. What do you think about that?"

"Rhiannon. It's time to go."

She blinked at him. "You must be upset. You just called me by my first name."

He stared at her for several seconds and then said, too softly, "Please."

She felt herself wavering, starting to feel like a spoiled, misbehaving child.

But no. She wasn't going to slink out of here just because Marcus Desmarais wanted her to. She didn't believe him about the weather. He was just saying that to get her to go.

The facts were simple. She wasn't doing anything wrong. The clock over the bar said it was just ten-thirty and she had every right to stay a little longer if she wanted to. Especially now that he'd tracked her down. Now that he was here, doing his precious duty, protecting her, if for any reason she happened to need protection—which she had not at any point thus far.

Her brother Alex knew where she was and that her bodyguard was with her and that meant no one at the Mc-Cade Ranch was worried about what might happen to her. There was no real reason she couldn't stay for just a bit.

"Marcus. Go and stand by the wall. I want to dance some more. I will let you know when I am ready to leave."

His face remained carved in stone while his eyes burned with green fury. He glared at her for a slow count of five and she became a little concerned that he would actually touch her, that he would manacle her arm with that big hand of his and drag her bodily from the premises. Sparks chased themselves beneath her skin at the very idea.

But he had iron control. In the end, he only turned sharply on his heel and went where she'd told him to go.


Marcus watched her.

It was all he was allowed to do, all she had permitted him to do.

Watch. As she danced with another cowboy. And another after that.

Frustration built. He wanted to grab her and throw her over his shoulder and carry her out of there bodily. But he could never do any such thing. She was his princess and he lived to serve her. And that meant, when it came right down to his will versus hers, she held all the cards.

No matter that a storm was brewing. No matter that all those cowboys she was dancing with were strangers. And she was beautiful and friendly and she gave her smiles to everyone.

There was going to be trouble with one of those strangers. One of them was bound to go too far as the evening wore on and the liquor kept flowing.

Then he would probably have to hurt someone. He didn't particularly look forward to that.

But then again, the more cowboys she danced with and the more he was forced to stand there and watch them put their common hands on her person, the more he felt heat building in his chest and behind his eyes, the more hurting someone began to seem like a good and necessary thing.

Rhia danced with yet another cowboy. It wasn't as much fun as it had been before Marcus appeared.

Somehow, with him there, observing her every move in that cold and disapproving way of his, no doubt judging her for not being a proper princess, it all seemed a bit tawdry. The pleasure had definitely gone out of her little adventure.

When the next cowboy stepped up to claim her, she thanked him, but said she was going to sit down for a while. She returned to the bar, where someone had bought her another tequila and a fresh beer.

Mona stepped up close. "Compliments of Bobby Dale," she said.

A few stools away, Bobby Dale raised his bottle of beer in a salute, grinning wide to reveal that space between his teeth.

Why not? She knocked back the shot and chugged the beer in a manner supremely unprincesslike. Somewhere in the shadows, Marcus was bound to be scowling in disgust.

She told herself she didn't care. Not in the least.

Bobby Dale signaled Mona to pour her another. The bartender had the shot poured before Rhia could stop her.

"Never mind about the beer," Rhia said. Without stopping to consider the wisdom of it, she picked up the shot glass and drained it.

Foolish. She knew that. The tequila made a fiery trail down the back of her throat and spread heat in her belly and she already regretted drinking it—and the one before it, too.

What was getting drunk going to prove? Nothing good. Plus, now she needed to pee.

She went to the ladies', where she had to wait for a stall. When she'd finished and was washing her hands, she saw that her hair was coming loose from its thick knot at the back of her head, her bangs were mussed and her lip gloss had long ago worn off. She looked way too much like she felt: forlorn and weary, a little bit woozy from those shots and the beer, with faint circles under her eyes.

She straightened her skirt and jacket, smoothed her bangs, repinned her hair, yanked her shoulders back and marched out the door. Of course, *he* was right there in the hallway, waiting for her.

One look at him, so stern and unwavering, patient as death, and she knew it was no good. The evening was over. It was time to go back to the Drop On Inn and try to get a few hours' sleep before boarding the family jet for home tomorrow.

Thanks to those shots and the beer, she shouldn't be driving. And she wouldn't. She would do the right thing and ride back with the man she'd tried so hard to get away from. Allie could have the rental people pick up the red truck tomorrow.

She looked directly at Marcus. "All right. You win. Let's go."

Without a word, he fell in behind her as she turned for the door.

"Hey, beautiful. Where you goin' in such an all-fired hurry?" Bobby Dale stepped in front of her. "Don't I at least get one little dance first?"

She felt Marcus moving closer behind her. There was no need. She could handle Bobby Dale. She put up a hand, warning Marcus back. "All right, Bobby Dale. One dance. And then I really do have to go."

Bobby didn't look drunk, exactly, but he didn't look quite sober, either. He bared the space between his teeth and narrowed his pale eyes at the silent man behind her. "Who's that? Your boyfriend?"

"No, he is not my boyfriend. Would you like that dance or not?"

"You bet I would, darlin'." He reached for her.

With some trepidation, she went into his arms.

Right away, she realized it was a mistake. He pulled her too close and whirled her away from the dance floor, into the shadows at the edges of the big barroom. When she stiffened and tried to put distance between his body and hers, he splayed a hand where he had no right to touch her and yanked her close again. "The minute I saw you, I knew you were special," he whispered in her ear, his breath reeking of stale beer. "All ladylike on the outside, hotter'n a bottle rocket underneath, just beggin' for the right man to set you off."

It was too much. "That's enough. Release me, now." Past Bobby's shoulder, Marcus appeared. She saw nothing but stillness and calm intent in his eyes. He was no more than a foot away.

Bobby Dale seemed to have no clue that Marcus was there. "Aw, now, sweetheart, don't go gettin' riled," Bobby whispered. He nuzzled her hair. "You and me got chemistry." Marcus reached out. "So you might as well—" Marcus touched Bobby's shoulder and Bobby stopped talking. The cowboy's mouth formed a round O and his eyes went flat. He let go of her, his arms dropping boneless to his sides as his knees crumpled and he collapsed to the floor.

Rhia blinked down at the unconscious cowboy, not really sure what had happened. "Is he…?"

"Ten minutes from now he'll be fine."

No one else in the bar seemed to have noticed. They were behind a pillar, just off the dance floor, out of the light.

And then, for the first time in eight years, Marcus touched her. She gasped as he took her in his arms and danced with her, turning her, moving both of them smoothly and swiftly toward the door.

She didn't argue. Beyond the fact that his touch had stunned her into silence, she was more than ready to leave Rowdy's Roadhouse behind. She only stared up into his haunting almost-green eyes and felt the deepest, saddest sense of longing. For *him*—a man who would hardly speak to her.

The longing made it all worse than ever. She looked in his distant eyes and saw herself: a complete disappointment, both as a princess *and* as a woman.

Marcus expected her to resist, to struggle free of his hold, to order him never, ever to lay a hand on her again. But she did none of those things. She let him dance her to the door and then when he released her only to grab her hand, she let him pull her along, out the door and down the steps, all without a single word.

It was snowing hard already and the wind was up. The sky overhead was starless, soot-gray, an anvil waiting to drop. He'd spent the worst of the winter in Elk Creek, providing security for Her Highness Arabella. He knew what was coming.

More snow. Probably a lot of it. The temperature was very cold and getting colder.

She staggered a little behind him and stared in a dazed way up at the sky. "You were right. It *is* snowing. It looks rather bad."

"Keep walking," he instructed. "The SUV is this way...."

She lowered her head and did what he'd told her to do. Her hand felt cool and small in his and he had to block out a few too-sweet memories of their forbidden weeks together at UCLA. During that time, they were always holding hands.

He led her down the middle row of vehicles. Since his arrival, the lot had thinned out a good deal. There were plenty of empty spaces now. Evidently, many of Rowdy's patrons had made their escape before the snow really started coming down. They passed the red pickup, the roof and bed of which were already wearing a mantle of white. And then, at last, they reached the SUV. He opened the backseat door for her and snow slid off the roof to plop at their feet.

She did jerk her hand free of his then. And she said one word, "No."

He had to actively resist his initial reaction, which was to scoop her up and put her in there bodily. "No, what, Rhiannon? No, you're not going, after all?"

She wrapped her arms around herself. She was shivering. "No, I'm not riding in back. I'll sit up in front, next to you."

It simply wasn't done, for Her Highness to ride in front with the driver. She knew that perfectly well.

But what did it matter at this point? If doing what was not done and sitting in front would get her into the vehicle, so be it. "All right. Hurry. We need to get on the road." He herded her around the front of the car, pulled open the passenger door for her and waited until she was safely inside. "Put on your seat belt," he said, and closed the door.

When he climbed in behind the wheel, she was shivering so hard that her teeth were chattering. He got the engine going and the heater running and then he backed out of the space and headed for the highway.

Something wasn't right.

And then it came to him. No one else was getting on the road. They had been the only ones leaving when they went out the door. No others seemed to have come out since then. The locals probably had the right idea. Those who hadn't left earlier were not going. They would wait out the worst of it.

He put his foot on the brake before pulling out of the parking lot and venturing onto the windblown, snow-thick highway. "It might be wiser to wait it out. Everyone else appears to be doing that."

She didn't look at him. She had her arms tightly wrapped around herself and her head scrunched down into her shoulders, like a turtle pulled into its shell. At least her shivering seemed to have abated a little. "No." She spoke softly. Without animosity, but with what seemed to him a deep and infinite sadness. "Please. Can we just go to Elk Creek? I couldn't bear to go back in there now."

He considered suggesting that they take rooms at the motel behind the roadhouse to wait out the storm. But she was in no condition to spend the night in some cheap motor lodge. The Drop On Inn was hardly the lap of luxury, but at least her family would be there, including her favorite sister, Alice. Sometimes Alice displayed bad judgment, but from what he knew of her, she had a good heart. Rhiannon trusted her absolutely and counted on her for support. It was a night when Rhiannon could probably use a little support.

"You're certain you want to risk the highway in this weather?" he asked one more time.

She nodded, still staring straight ahead. "Please. Let's just go."

So off they went.

The snow came down harder. And the wind blew the thick whiteness horizontally, straight at the windshield. He drove slowly, with care.

But it was bad and getting worse. Almost immediately, visibility went from poor to practically nothing. He started thinking about suggesting again that it would be safer to turn around and go back. But by now he wasn't sure if that actually *would* be safer. He couldn't see the shoulder on either side of the road. And if another vehicle appeared while he was trying to turn…

He kept going forward. The wipers labored to clear the snow from the glass. Rhiannon sat beside him, silent. And very still.

She would be all right. Of course she would. She was a strong and admirable woman with a core of steel. He just needed to get her back to safety with her family and everything would be all right. Just needed to…

Rhiannon gasped.

Another car had appeared, coming on way too fast in the opposite direction. He couldn't actually see the vehicle yet. Just four blinding lights: a pair of headlights and another pair higher up, the kind the local ranchers sometimes mounted above the windshield.

"Marcus!" Rhia whispered low. "Oh, my God…"

"It's all right," he told her, though she had to know that it wasn't.

"Marcus, I'm so sorry. So sorry about everything…."

"Shh," he soothed. And lied again. "It's all right." He leaned on the horn.

But it did no good.

The four blinding beams of light started turning. All at once, they illuminated the far side of the road as the vehicle itself appeared, a brown pickup skidding sideways, no longer in the opposite lane but straight ahead in theirs and sliding fast right for them.

Marcus saw the driver in the pickup's side window. An old fellow in a straw cowboy hat, eyes like two black holes, mouth agape.

There was only one choice and Marcus took it. He turned the wheel sharply toward the shoulder. The pickup whipped by, clipping them in the rear as it went, causing a bone-jarring second of impact, but then skidding on, vanishing into the maelstrom behind them.

He tried to swerve the wheel back into the lane. But it was no good. The snow-thick, icy road surface provided no purchase. The SUV kept going, right over the bank and off the road.

## Chapter Four

Rhia's spinning mind couldn't keep up with the crash as it happened. She saw the brown truck skidding sideways at them, the face of a terrified old man in a big hat. And then, all at once they were over the side of the road, the front of the SUV suddenly pointing straight down. She closed her eyes, braced herself and waited to die as they dropped off the edge of the cliff.

But it wasn't a cliff, after all.

They hit bottom almost instantly, the nose of the SUV coming up a little and leveling out, the impact stunning enough to send a jolt of pure agony singing up her spine. A giant fluffy wall appeared, came straight at her and smacked her in the face and chest. It was already deflating when she realized it was the air bag.

By then, the SUV had stopped moving. The only sounds were the creaks and the cracking and strange airy sighs of a vehicle that would probably never be drivable again.

"Rhia. My God…" Marcus was half out of his seat, bending close to her. "Rhia, are you…?"

She dared to reach out, to touch his dear, forbidden face. Real. Warm. A little rough with a day's worth of beard, just she remembered it in her lonely, tortured dreams. "You just called me Rhia…" He'd never called her that, not since their brief time together. It was unacceptable for him to call her by her full first name. But to call her Rhia was, for him, beyond the pale.

"My God," he said again. "Are you injured?"

She closed her eyes, ran a quick physical inventory. When she opened them, she dared a nervous smile. "No. I'm all right. Pretty shaken up, but all right."

"Thank God."

"You?"

"Fine," he said quickly, dismissing his own condition the way he always dismissed everything concerning his well-being.

She thought of the other driver then, and stiffened.

"What is it?" he demanded. "What hurts? Tell me."

"That poor old man in the truck…" She reached over and unhooked her seat belt. "We have to get out, go to him. That pickup must have crashed."

"Wait."

"But, Marcus…"

"I'll call for an ambulance." He spoke to the thing in his ear. "Call nine-one-one." She waited anxiously for him to ask for an ambulance. But a moment later, he pulled his cell phone from his pocket and checked the display.

"What?" she demanded.

He looked at her again. "No signal. Must be the storm."

"Oh, no…"

He put the phone away and rehooked his seat belt. "Put your belt back on."

She did what he asked. "What are you going to do?"

"See if I can get us going again, get us out of this ditch."

It could be possible, couldn't it? The headlights were still working. They gleamed strangely, half buried in the snowbank the vehicle had scraped up like a plow as they hit the ditch. The windshield and windows were still intact. The front end looked pretty bad, though, all crooked and crumpled.

Marcus reached around his deflated air bag and started the car.

Or he tried to. All he raised was a click, after which the headlights went dark.

The whites of his eyes gleamed at her through the shadows. "Don't worry. I'll try again." He did. Another click. And again. More clicking, but not even a hint of a response from the engine.

"Uh-oh," she said softly. And she thought of that poor old cowboy again. "Marcus. We have to get out of this vehicle and get back up to the road. We have to make sure that man is all right."

He regarded her steadily through the gloom. "You're shivering."

The engine wasn't working—and that meant neither was the heater. She wrapped her arms around herself and ordered her teeth not to chatter. "It's nothing. I am fine."

His iron jaw was set. "Your high-heeled shoes are made of satin and you don't have a coat."

She despised herself right then. Stuck in a snowbank without proper gear. An old man could die because she'd just *had* to get away from the man sitting next to her. "I'm sorry, so sorry. It's all my fault. I know that. But we have to do something. At least we have to see if there's anything we *can* do."

He reached over the back of the seat and came up with

a lap blanket. "Wrap this around you." He shoved it at her. "I didn't hear a crash, so it could be that that cowboy regained control of his pickup."

"How could we have heard a crash? *We* were crashing."

He put up both hands. "Don't argue. Just wrap the blanket around you." He undid his belt again, reached across her, popped her belt open for the second time then slid the blanket behind her and closed it around her.

She stared into those eyes that would forever fill her lonely dreams, breathed in his still-remembered scent: plain soap, all man. "But, Marcus—"

"I will go, all right?"

"Oh, Marcus…"

"Take the blanket." He drew one of her hands from the warm folds. "Hold it close around you…."

She did what he said. He let go of her and she felt absurdly bereft. Then he told her again, in an even, calming sort of tone, "I will go. I will go and check and see if there's anything I can do." He slid over to the backseat so smoothly, she didn't realize what he was doing until he was behind her.

Bewildered, she turned to stare at him over her shoulder. Was it those tequila shots she'd foolishly drunk at Rowdy's? The accident? This whole awful day with Marcus right there every time she turned around, reminding her so cruelly of everything they would never have?

Probably all of the above. But whatever the reason, her brain seemed to be working as if in a fog, her reactions all out of whack, delayed. Wrong.

She'd pushed him to go out there and see about the old man. But now that he had said he would go, she suddenly realized how very foolish that would be. "Wait. No, I… That's not right. You can't go alone. It's a blizzard out there and it's not safe…."

He was bending over the floor of the backseat by then. But he stopped what he was doing and straightened enough that his shadowed gaze found hers. "We need to go see about that cowboy who almost ran us over. You *can't* go, you have to see that. So that leaves me. But now you don't want me to go. Make up your mind. Please."

What mind? "I..." She stared at him hopelessly. He let out a long breath and bent over the backseat floor again. She kicked off her ruined shoes, shoved the air bag aside and drew her feet up under her, hoarding her body's warmth.

He straightened again and light filled the cab.

She blinked. "A flashlight? Where did that come from?"

He dropped another blanket over the seat. "Put this around your legs and feet."

She hastened to do what he instructed. "But where...?"

"There's an emergency kit under the floor back here. Another blanket, a second flashlight, jumper cables, flares, a thermal tarp, things like that."

"It...came with the vehicle?"

"For a price. You know your brother."

Alexander. Of course. She should have realized. Alex was extremely security- and safety-conscious—almost scarily so. "I don't suppose there's a pair of size seven and a half women's snow boots and a nice down jacket?"

"Dream on." In the weird, slanting beam of the flashlight, she saw his mouth twitch. Good Lord, he had almost smiled. If things weren't so dire, that would have done her heart good.

"Marcus."

"What now?"

"I've changed my mind. I don't want you to go out there."

"Is that a command?"

"Oh, don't be ridiculous." She huffed out a hard breath and drew the blankets closer around her.

His gaze stayed locked on hers. Level. Unwavering. "It was an honest question."

"Can we just…dispense with all that, at least until we're safely back at the motor lodge?"

He considered. "Fair enough. Then *I* will decide. And I think it's best if I try to get up to the road, at least. I'll set some flares." He held them up. "And I'll see if that brown pickup is anywhere nearby—and if it is, I'll see if there's anything I can do for the driver."

She knew he was right in what he planned to do, even though she longed to beg him not to do it. "You won't go far?"

"No. My main responsibility is you, to keep you safe and well. You're the priority." She was so grateful to hear him say that—at the same time as she felt deeply ashamed to have gotten them into this awful situation. She had behaved badly on any number of levels and her evening of adventure had somehow gotten completely out of control. She sent a little prayer to heaven that God would be merciful and protect the man who was only trying to protect *her*. He added, "I'll stay well to the shoulder and I won't get out of sight of the flares that I set."

She took a slower, deeper breath. "Yes. All right."

He tried his phone one more time. "Dead air," he said softly. He flicked the door lock beside him. The front door on the driver's side was jammed against the bank, but the back door looked as though it might have some play. He pulled the handle and put his rocklike shoulder into it. With much crunching and groaning, the door slowly opened. It didn't open far. Too soon it was lodged in the snow on the bank. Freezing air swirled in. "Stay bundled up," he said. "I'll be back soon." And with that, he slipped out into the storm.

"Be safe," she whispered, as he wrestled the door free of the snowbank and pushed it shut behind him.

She stared over the seat, tracking the flashlight's glow as he slogged away from the car. He began to climb the bank. Too soon, she lost the light—and him. The view through the rear window was a narrow one from the front seat.

That was unbearable—to have lost sight of him so soon. She scrambled over the seat and then over *that* seat so she could look out the back. From there, she could see a faint glow up on the road. "Please, please God, keep him safe…." She had to resist the urge to bargain with the Almighty. She'd been foolish enough in the past few hours. She wasn't going to start trying to make deals with God.

Through the swirling haze of the snow, she saw a flash of sizzling brightness, followed by the red glow of a flare. Then came a second flash and there were two. The flares lit the upper rim of the ditch. His flashlight beam began moving along the shoulder, back the way they had come.

Too soon, the flashlight's glow was swallowed by the storm. She had only the red gleam of the flares to comfort her while she waited.

And waited. As far as she could tell no other cars had passed. She saw only the light given off by the flares. She didn't know what time it was. She wore no watch, had no phone with her. She had no idea if the car's clock might be working. And she wasn't about to scramble back over the seats to find out, wasn't about to stop staring out that back window, *willing* his return.

A glad cry escaped her when she saw the flashlight's glow again. It seemed to take form out of the spinning snow, materializing slowly from the whirl of whiteness.

It was coming closer, thank God. And it had probably only been ten or fifteen minutes since the beam had been swallowed by the storm. But somehow, those minutes had seemed like several lifetimes strung end to end.

At the bank, the light paused. There was the flash of another flare as a third warning torch lit up between the first two.

And then, at last, he began to descend the bank.

She scrambled back over the seat so she could push the door open for him when he reached it. The cold air and snow swirled in along with the big, cold man and the glow of the trusty flashlight. He pulled the door shut and she backed away to the far side of the seat in order to quell the powerful need to throw her arms around him and hold on tight.

"You're safe," she whispered prayerfully. "Oh, and I'll bet you're freezing cold...."

He turned off the light, set it aside and brushed snow from his shoulders, stomped it off his boots. She watched the shadowed, eagerly awaited shape of him as her eyes once again grew accustomed to the gloom.

Resignedly, he muttered, "Didn't I tell you to stay bundled up in the front seat?"

She laughed, a slightly hysterical sound. "I did stay bundled up. You never said a word about the front seat— and did you find him, the old man?"

"No. Not a sign of him or the pickup." He brushed snow off his hair.

Cold droplets touched her cheek. She swiped them away. "But...how could that be possible?"

"The snow's falling fast, covering our tracks. But the ones where he skidded sideways in our lane were so deep, they were still visible. I followed them—until they seemed to straighten out."

"Straighten out?" She considered the impossibility of that. "Surely you're joking."

"No."

"You're saying he somehow pulled out of that horrible slide?"

"It looks that way."

"Incredible."

"I told you. People who live here are used to driving in bad weather."

"He wasn't doing a very good job of it when he came flying at us."

Those big shoulders lifted in a shrug. "What can I tell you? It looked to me like he pulled out of it somehow." He wrapped his hands around himself and rubbed his arms.

"You're freezing," she said softly.

"I'll warm up, don't worry."

"Oh, please. It's almost as cold in here as it is out there." Cold and getting colder. Her nose felt like a small slab of ice. She gathered her feet underneath her and wrapped the blankets tighter. It had been a little chilly, even that morning, so she'd worn lacy tights, though she'd been tempted to go without them. Now, she was very grateful for at least that one good choice she'd made in a day and evening of really bad ones.

He tried his phone again. "Nothing," he told her after a minute.

"What time is it? Do you know?"

He pulled back the sleeves of the jacket and sweatshirt to reveal one of those military-style multifunction watches. "Twelve-forty."

She shivered a little. "Already tomorrow..." She watched as he bent and got the other blanket from the kit under the floor and settled it around himself. "You mentioned there's a thermal tarp in there, too."

He tugged the blanket closer, hunching his head down into the soft folds. "And?"

"You should use it, get your body temperature back up."

He just sat there, a large dark lump in the murky dimness of the cab. Annoyance nipped at her. The man made denial of his own basic comfort into something an art form. Just because she had gotten them into this mess didn't mean he had to freeze to death before help came.

And then he did bend over again. He brought out the tarp, which resembled nothing so much as a much-folded slab of aluminum foil. It caught what little ambient light there was and gleamed silver. "Here. You use it. You need to stay bundled up until help comes."

She made no move to take it. "You need it more than I do."

"Take it, Rhiannon."

She looked away. "How long will the flares last?"

"Rhiannon."

Slowly, she turned her head to face his shadowed form once more. She asked again, "The flares?"

He was still holding out the tarp. When she only sat where she was, unmoving, waiting for him to answer her, he dropped it onto the seat between them. "I don't know. Up to an hour, possibly."

"And if help doesn't come by then?"

"It will come eventually. The storm will end. In the morning, they'll have searchers looking for us. We're on a much-traveled highway and there will be vehicles we can flag down as soon as the road is passable again. We only need to keep warm until they find us."

She looked at him for a long time. Then she dared to say it. "We need to share our body heat. We need to share the blankets and the tarp."

He sat very still. She felt the intense regard of his gaze

through the gloom. Finally, he admitted it, too. "You're right."

They moved simultaneously. He picked up the tarp and started opening it. She helped. It was big, much bigger than the blankets.

When it was fully opened and billowed out over both seats, he said, "I'll sit back against the door. You sit between my legs. We can wrap two blankets and the tarp around both of us. You can take the third blanket for extra protection on your legs and feet."

It was a good plan—as much as it covered. "What about *your* feet?"

"No problem."

She peered toward the floor. She couldn't see his boots. It was too dark down there. But she had a very strong feeling that they were soaked through. "Are those boots waterproof?"

"They're fine."

"Wrong answer. You can't sit here all night with wet feet. You'll get frostbite."

"I'm all right."

"Oh, stop it. As soon as the storm ends, you're going to want to get out and stand on the side of the road to flag someone down. You won't be able to do that if your feet are frozen. But if you take off the boots and get your feet under the blankets and tarp, our body heat will dry your socks—all of which is completely obvious, and you know that it is."

He said with exceeding grimness, "You keep talking about body heat."

She didn't know whether to laugh or cry. He sounded so discouraged. Weary to the core. She felt bad about that— really bad. "Listen, Marcus. I mean this sincerely. I am very sorry about what's happened and I know that it's all my fault. I know the last thing you want to do is to share body heat with me."

"There. You just said it again."

"I'm sorry. Again. But it has to be done."

"And you have no idea what I want." His voice was deeper than ever. Rough in that delicious way she remembered from long ago.

Her silly heart got all fluttery. She commanded it to settle down. "We have to do this."

"Yes," he said. "I know."

"So take off those boots."

"All right." He lifted a foot.

"Here. Let me help."

He sent her one of those glances. Even through the dark, she could read it. She knew just what he was thinking. *It is not done for Your Highness to help a mere bodyguard off with his boots.*

But then he surprised her and swung one wet boot her way. She let go of her blankets, took the boot in both hands, by the wet toe and the soggy heel, and removed it, after which he offered her the other one. She took it off, too.

Yes, it did seem a very intimate thing to be doing for him. And it made her so sad all over again, made her think of those beautiful weeks all those years ago, when she was in her first year as an art major and he was only twenty-two, in California for a special Montedoran fellowship, a two-month intensive course of study in behavioral sciences, leadership and military psychology.

They'd met when he saw her in the student bookstore and recognized her. She'd caught him staring at her and boldly demanded to know what he thought he was looking at.

Her young heart had skipped a beat when he saluted.

"Your Highness, Sub-Lieutenant Marcus Desmarais of the Sovereign's Guard at your service."

She'd laughed in delight to find a countryman at UCLA. And she'd invited him to get some coffee with her. He'd surprised both of them and accepted her invitation.

They'd quickly become friends. It had seemed such a natural thing, with both of them so far from home. Their innate understanding of each other as Montedorans had seemed greater there than their differences. The chasm between them, he a commoner and she a princess, hadn't mattered at all.

At least not to her.

To her, it had never mattered. After all, her mother ruled her country—and *she* had married a commoner, an American actor from Texas. It was a wonderfully success-ful marriage. Born the last of her line to rule a principal-ity crushed under the weight of massive debt, Adrienne Bravo-Calabretti had given her husband and her country four princes and five princesses. Under her mother's rule, with her father's unwavering support, Montedoro had pros-pered. The country was rich now. The throne had an heir and plenty of spares.

*That* was what had come of a princess marrying a com-moner.

Rhia dropped the second boot to the floor and wished the man sitting there in the dark beside her could be as open-minded and far-seeing as her own father had always been.

"Come here," Marcus said. "You're shivering again."

With a sigh, Rhia turned and positioned herself between his hard thighs. They arranged the blankets into a nest to shelter them. She wrapped one of them around her feet and legs as he'd instructed. The others he drew around him and thus around them both, with the thermal tarp on top as he settled back against the door.

The tarp was big enough to cover them completely, wrapping around their bodies with plenty to tuck snugly over their legs and feet. He enveloped her in his big arms and pulled her back against his broad chest.

Instantly, she felt warmer, comforted. Safe. But how comfortable was he? "What about your back?"

"It's fine."

"But isn't it cold, against the door like that?"

"Rhiannon. It's fine." He held her even closer. It felt so good. She tried not to enjoy it too awfully much. His warm breath stirred her hair as he added downright cheerfully, "I'm feeling quite toasty, as a matter of fact."

"Toasty." She allowed herself a smile.

"Try to get some rest."

"Is it still snowing?" She struggled to sit higher, to see out the back window, rubbing against him intimately as she moved.

He made a low sound, quickly quelled. It might have been the beginnings of a groan. His big arms tightened, holding her still. "Stay here. Stay warm." His deep, wonderful voice rumbled against her back and lower down she felt...him. Heat flooded her cheeks as she realized that her wriggling about to see out the back window had aroused him.

She gulped and tried to sit still and reminded herself he couldn't see her blush. It was too dark and she had her back to him. She cleared her throat. "I just wanted to see if it was still snowing."

"It is."

"Has it let up any?"

"No. Rest."

She didn't think she could sleep. No way. This was too

strange and wonderful. It was…like all her forbidden fantasies somehow come to life: the two of them, in the darkness, all wrapped up together, nice and tight.

Yes, she felt a bit embarrassed at the thick, hard ridge of him pressing low against her back.

But she also felt…excited by it. Glad. To have such basic, undeniable proof that he still desired her, after all these years. That he wasn't as indifferent to her as he always tried to make her believe. It was a petty sort of triumph and she knew that.

She ordered herself to stop being smug. The man couldn't help his biological response, what with her all smashed up against his private parts like this. His physical arousal proved nothing—except that he was a man and she was a woman. He had done his duty by her tonight, and then some. She would be thankful for that and behave better in the future.

Her body slowly relaxed. Now that her teeth were no longer chattering, she could actually almost feel optimistic.

Yes, it had been an awful experience, all told. But there was a bright side. Neither of them had been injured. It appeared the old cowboy in the brown pickup had somehow escaped unscathed. And as soon as the snow stopped and daylight came, they would be rescued.

It could have been so much worse.

And she really was exhausted. She closed her eyes and rested her head back against the steady, sure beating of his heart.

Her eyes drifted shut.

And she remembered….

## Chapter Five

Two weeks.

That was all it took in the easy, casual atmosphere of Southern California. Two weeks far from everything that defined them as worlds apart, and what began as friendship became a love affair.

A *secret* affair. Rhia was barely eighteen, after all. She told herself it was a fling, that she was much too young to settle down. And Marcus was a military man to the core, ruled by duty. He considered himself beneath her and felt more than a little guilty that he was her first lover—that he was her lover at all.

He told her more than once that he knew she deserved a prince. But in those magical, perfect days, he actually opened up to her, even relaxed with her. He told her of his childhood. He was raised by the nuns at St. Stephen's Orphanage. They'd found him as a newborn on the steps of Montedoro's oldest church, the Cathedral of Our Lady of

Sorrows. He didn't know who his people were, not his father, not his mother. He'd started his life with no one, and then been adopted as an infant.

"But the couple divorced. I was the glue that was supposed to hold them together. When I didn't do the job, neither of them wanted me. It was back to St. Stephen's when I was three. After that, I was a very, very good little boy— for the nuns. But evidently, I made sure none of the others who came looking for a child chose me. I don't remember how, exactly, I was so small. But I know even now that I didn't need that kind of heartache all over again."

She had told him she admired him, for what he'd suffered, for how he had managed to grow up both strong and good.

And he had captured her face in his two big hands. "Not so good. Not strong at all. If I were strong and good, I wouldn't be here with you now."

They stood out on the grass by the large and beautiful neo-Romanesque style undergraduate library. She remembered thick trees, dappled shadows, a feeling that they were the only two people in the world right then. She went on tiptoe, kissed him. "No regrets. None. I am very, very glad you're here."

And right then, he made her promise that they would walk away in the end, that it would be over forever once he finished his fellowship and returned to Montedoro. That the time they had together would be their secret. "Promise me, Rhia. When I go, we cut it clean. And no one else will ever know."

"Yes. Of course. I promise." She had nodded, beaming happily up at him, aglow with what she honestly believed at that time was a lovely mingling of warm friendship and delicious desire. She agreed to it ending, to it being their secret. She was so sure at the time that cutting it clean when he left was what she wanted. Not because he was "just" a soldier, but because she was only eighteen and had her whole life ahead of her and had never imagined she might find her true love in her first year of college.

At UCLA, they both stayed in dorm rooms, in separate halls. He had three roommates and she had one. They couldn't be together in their rooms.

When they decided they *would* be together—*really* be together—they had found a small, inexpensive hotel not far from the campus. It was beautiful to her, that hotel. In the Spanish style, with thick stucco walls and a red tile roof, all on one level, with each room more like a tiny apartment opening onto a central walkway than a hotel room.

La Casa de la Luna, the place was called.

The house of the moon.

She loved it there, in their own special house of the moon. One room in particular, the one they used the very first time, became "their" room. Their room had bright bougainvillea climbing the white wall outside the window and twin birds of paradise flanking the door. Their room had a small sitting area where they sometimes studied together. The bathroom had an old claw-footed tub and the mirror over the sink was streaked with age.

It was a magical place, their room. Every time they visited, she wished they might never have to leave. And when they did leave, she lived only for when they would go there again. But he was in America for only two months and that time flew by on swift wings.

They parted as planned. She drove him to LAX and kissed him goodbye and managed not to cry. As he left her to go through security, his broad back so straight and proud, never once turning to see if she was still there watching him go, she reminded herself that this was what she wanted. Their time together had been so beautiful. And now they would both move on.

Too bad she couldn't seem to forget him. Too bad no other man ever seemed to measure up....

"Marcus?" Her voice, soft. Tentative.

He stirred from hazy dreams where he was hard and aching and she was pressed tight against him. He couldn't push her away. He had, for some reason unclear to him but urgent, to keep her close, to hold her in his arms. He couldn't push her away.

But he couldn't kiss her, either. Couldn't take away all her clothes and bury himself in her velvety heat....

That was forbidden.

That could never be again.

It was torture of the most unbearable kind. And every soldier knew how it went when you were tortured. If your tormentor was good enough, eventually, you would give it all up—betray your family, your country, all you held dear.

Just to make the agony stop.

"Marcus?"

He blinked, opened his eyes to darkness.

And remembered. Her Highness Arabella's wedding. Rowdy's Roadhouse. The crash.

Rhia actually *was* pressed against him. His dream of being tortured endlessly by an unflagging state of arousal was real.

"Are you awake?" she asked.

"I am now," he grumbled and set his mind to blocking out the ache in his groin.

Wrapped in their cocoon of blankets and the tarp, they were warm, and that was what mattered. His socks were already dry and he didn't have to worry about her getting frostbite or pneumonia—or worse, freezing to death before rescue came.

"The snow?" she asked.

He peered over the seat. "Looks like it's still coming down."

"What time is it?"

He freed his arm long enough to look at his watch. "Ten to two."

"Your phone?"

He tried the headset. "Still out. Go to sleep. In a few hours, this will all be over."

She didn't do what he asked her to do. But then, she rarely had. "I have a confession," she whispered.

"Save it for a priest."

She made a low sound in her throat. A soft sound. A sexy sound. A sound that seemed to go straight to his tortured privates. "I told Alice about us. She's known for eight years. One week after I dropped you off at LAX, I called her and told her everything."

He wasn't surprised. "That wasn't wise."

"She would never tell anyone. She never has."

God in heaven, she felt good in his arms. And she smelled so good, like vanilla and jasmine flowers and something else, something that was only her. He would know her in the darkest part of the blackest night, in the crush of a crowd, blindfolded. "Rest."

"You keep saying that."

He almost pressed a kiss into her dark, fragrant hair. But he caught himself just in time. "We have to sit here like this to stay warm. We might as well get some rest."

"Or we could talk."

"There is nothing to talk about."

"Liar." She said it very low. And vehemently. "You are such a liar, Marcus."

He didn't argue. She was right. He had told the lies that he *had* to tell. And he had no intention of digging into the truth tonight.

Or ever.

She let out a sad little sigh. "We have so very much to talk about. If only you would."

"No, we don't."

She was silent then. Which was good. They only needed to get through this night without doing something foolish, without saying all the things that were too dangerous to say. Then they could both return to their separate and very different lives. Which was as it should be.

He rested his head back against the ice-cold side window and told himself to sleep, to block out the soft, tempting, never-forgotten shape of the woman in his arms—and not, under any circumstances, to think about the past....

Marcus did sleep.

And he dreamed about the things that he'd sworn not to think of.

He dreamed of that time six years ago, when she came home to Montedoro before her junior year at college and sought him out.

Somehow, she had learned his private email address. Three emails she sent him. He didn't respond to the first two. He consigned them to the trash and told himself that the wisest response to her was no response at all.

He never should have presumed even to speak with her in California. But something so impossible had happened the day before. And he was still reeling from it, his whole world tilted sideways, off its axis. Gone completely wrong.

She had challenged him and he had dared to respond as an equal might.

And after that, somehow he couldn't walk away—didn't

*want* to walk away. Not right then. He wanted to be with her, even though such a thing was completely forbidden.

To be her friend for that brief time had been unacceptable. To be her lover?

It was so much more than wrong. It was a desecration of all he held sacred. He owed everything to her family. Her Sovereign Highness Adrienne was a fair and just ruler, and a generous one. She truly cared for the lowliest of her subjects. She helped to fund St. Stephen's. And every year at Christmastime, Her Sovereign Highness would visit. She would come bearing gifts for each and every orphaned child and she would personally speak with every child who was old enough to form a recognizable sentence. Every year from the year he was three and his adoptive parents returned him to the orphanage like a defective toy, the sovereign princess spoke with him. And every year, she seemed to remember the things he had said the year before.

When he was six, he told her he wanted to be a soldier for his country, to join the guard, to serve the princely family. Her Sovereign Highness took him at his word. He received the education he needed. He began to train for the Sovereign's Guard at eighteen. But even before that, he was taken under the wing of Sir Hector Anteros, who was then the captain of the guard. Sir Hector was the closest thing to a real father that Marcus had ever known and Hector had seen to it that his protégé received an officer's commission after graduating from the University of Montedoro at the age of twenty-one. Marcus was no one, a foundling. And yet, because of Princess Adrienne, the future he'd only barely dared to dream of was his.

Essentially, Marcus owed the princely family his life, his education, his relationship with the man who paved the way for him and his livelihood. And he had repaid their endless kindness by seducing one of their daughters.

So yes. When Rhiannon sent him those first two emails six years ago, he had pretended that he didn't receive them. But then came the third email in which she threatened to seek him out in person, to come to the barracks not far from the palace where he lived and demand to speak with him. At that point, he'd agreed to meet with her in secret.

She chose the place. It was a short drive out of Montedoro, in the French countryside, a deserted farmhouse that belonged to her family. He arrived first.

He was standing on the front step, wondering if she had come to her senses and decided to stay away, after all, when a small yellow sports car appeared racing toward him along the dusty front lane. She pulled up a few feet from the steps and got out.

Her coffee-brown hair gleamed in the summer sun. She wore a sleeveless red cotton dress and she stood by the car and looked up the steps at him and he was in hell. Wanting to run to her, to reach for her, needing the feel of her flesh beneath his hands in the same way he needed to suck in his next breath.

And knowing that taking her in his arms could not, under any circumstances, be allowed to happen. Touching her would be too dangerous. Once he had his hands on her again, he might never be able to let her go.

He saw in those big dark eyes that she was going to say things that could never be unsaid. And so he had stood there, in the shade of the olive tree by the padlocked door of that plain farmhouse, and listened to her say those things.

"I think…I love you, Marcus. I think we made a giant mistake, to end it the way we did. I think of you often. All the time. It's as though you're somehow inside my heart. Here." She laid her slim hand above her breast. "As though you're somehow in my blood. Don't you…ever think about me? Don't you ever think you might want to try again?"

And then he said the lies he had to say. "No. I'm sorry. I don't want to try again. I'm content, I promise you, with the agreement we made two years ago. I wish you well. And now, would you please get back in that little yellow car and drive away and never try to contact me again?"

"But, Marcus…" She spoke gently. Carefully. Her enormous eyes beckoned him down to drowning. "Don't you ever even wonder if we might have made a mistake? Don't you ever wish or imagine that it could be different for you and me?"

"No," he said, again, his tone as deliberate, as carefully controlled as hers. "The mistake was on my part, to have ever dared to touch you or even to speak with you."

"But, Marcus, that's not what I meant."

He put up a hand. "Please. Hear me. The mistake was not that we ended it. The mistake was that it ever started in the first place. All I want from you, ma'am, is for you to keep the promise you made to me two years ago."

She had stood there, so beautiful it ripped his heart in two to look at her, and she had cried. "'Ma'am.' Oh, you can't be serious. Ma'am?"

"I would like for you to go now."

"Oh, God." She stood there in the dirt drive and stretched out her hands to him. "Please, Marcus. Please. Won't you just give us a chance?" The tears tracked down her soft cheeks, dripped over her chin. "I miss you. So much. Couldn't we just talk it over, at least, just… Oh, Marcus. Don't do this, don't just send me away."

But he had to. In time, he knew, she would thank him for it.

He made himself stand there, still and straight as any

statue. "You must go, ma'am. There is nothing more that I can say."

She stared at him through red, wet eyes for an endless moment. And then, with a ragged sob, she buried her face in her hands. He stood there, frozen to the spot, knowing that to move so much as a centimeter would destroy his control and have him running to her, grabbing her close. So he didn't move. He stayed where he was and he watched her slim shoulders shake as she strove to collect herself.

After forever, she dashed away the last of her tears, wiped her arm across her running nose and drew her shoulders tall to face him again. "I think you're a coward, Marcus." Her voice was cold now, frosty with disdain, though her swollen, red eyes remained turbulent, shining with the last of her tears.

He didn't speak, didn't move. He only waited, *willing* her to go.

"All right, then," she said at last. "Goodbye."

He watched her turn from him, hating himself for the pain he had brought her, a really bad emptiness in the center of his chest—and yet, even then, certain that it was the right thing he was doing. She got in the car and drove away.

And that was it. The end of it.

In real life, anyway.

But in this dream he seemed to be having, the ending at the farmhouse steps was…changing.

Morphing into something altogether different.

In this dream, he was hard. Aching for her. In this dream, she turned to the yellow car, as before. She pulled open the door, as before.

And then she pushed it shut again.

Not as before.

Everything went haywire then. She whirled and came to him, racing up the steps, her face flushed, still swollen from her fit of weeping, her dark hair coming loose from its pins, falling to curl around her unforgettable face. "Tell me again," she demanded. "Tell me how you want me to go...."

And it was too much.

Pure need took over. He reached for her. She came to him, sighing, twisting in his arms. He realized she'd been facing away from him, leaning against him. But now she had turned, so she lay against him face-to-face, her soft breasts smashed against his chest, her warm breath flowing across the flesh of his throat.

And suddenly, they were on some narrow padded surface inside the locked, deserted farmhouse. It was dark and cold in there, but they had their body heat to keep each other warm, a tent of blankets to shelter them.

She kissed him, her mouth opening, a night-blooming flower, under his, her breath flowing into him, their tongues meeting again, at last, after an eternity of loneliness and denial. He stroked her tongue with his, caressing, touching all those secret, wet, slick surfaces beyond her parted lips.

His arms were filled with her, so warm and soft and perfectly made. And so very eager. Her hair tumbled down, tangling around them, a dark web of curling silk.

So real, the taste of her. Nothing an ordinary soldier like him should ever be allowed to know. Honey. Ambrosia. The food of the gods. She tasted of all the things he had no right to touch. She tasted of paradise.

Real.

So real...

Better than all the hungry, lonely, longing dreams of her in all the years since...

She gasped.

And she wiggled against him, driving him wild, as she

slid her arms up his chest and used her soft, slim hands to frame his face.

"Marcus. Marcus, are you *asleep?*" Asleep? He tried to capture her mouth again, but she retreated, though her soft hands still held him, one on either cheek. "Marcus." Her voice was sweetly scolding now.

Awareness dawned: the heat between them, the hard door at his back. The cold just beyond their tent of blankets and tarp....

It seemed so real because it *was* real.

He opened his eyes. She was right there, her eyes waiting, shining at him through the dark.

"Sweet holy virgin," he heard himself whisper.

She moved, her body shifting a little between his legs, reminding him sharply all over again of how much he wanted her. He stifled a groan of need as she said, "And here I thought you had finally admitted you just *had* to make love with me...."

She was right. He had done exactly that, more or less. In his dreams.

Literally.

"Rhiannon, I..." He had no idea what to say.

She leaned closer again, sliding against him, stroking him with that fine body of hers. He gritted his teeth, absolutely certain he was going to lose it any second now. Her soft lips just barely brushed his. "I have a question."

He made a sound, a helpless, yearning, croaking sound.

Her lips moved against his. He felt the whisper of her warm breath across his mouth, over his cheek. "It's been a terrible night, Marcus. Worst of the worst."

"Er." Again, he had to swallow a groan. "That was a question?"

"I'm getting there."

Yet another tortured sound escaped him.

And she said, "My question is, *why not?*"

He didn't have to ask why not what. He knew exactly why not what.

She stroked the stubble-rough side of his face and whispered softly, in a voice of purest temptation, "Why not go ahead with it? Why not do what neither of us can stop wanting to do, just one more time?"

He knew exactly how he should respond to those dangerous questions. He needed to take her by the shoulders and put her gently but firmly away from him. But instead, he muttered in a rough, choked growl, "It would be…wrong."

She used the backs of her fingers to stroke the close-clipped hair at his temples. "I don't care, Marcus. I really don't care if it's wrong. I only want one good thing to remember about tonight, one sweet, naughty secret to make it…not quite so awful. I thoroughly understand that it's never going to be, between you and me. That it's over and it's *been* over. For years and years."

He tried to speak.

She put her soft hand between them and covered his mouth with her palm. "Shh. Not finished." He gulped and nodded. She took her hand away and brought her lips close to his once more. "But tonight, well, it's all been a complete and utter disaster. And now, here we are, waiting for the storm to end so that we can go our separate ways, waiting for the morning, keeping each other warm. And I say that now, tonight, is the only opportunity we're ever going to get to be together one more time. I say that the way you were kissing me just a few minutes ago, even if you *were* half-asleep, proves that you wouldn't mind doing exactly what I'm suggesting." She rocked her hips against him then—to prove her point, he supposed. And she did prove it. He groaned out loud that time. He couldn't stop himself. And she made a low, triumphant little sound. "*Yes*. That's what *I* say, Marcus. Yes. You and me. Tonight, right now. One more time...."

He exerted a superhuman effort of will and said, "We cannot. It's too dangerous. I've brought nothing to protect you." She knew his stand on contraception. He'd grown up without a father *or* a mother. He was adamant that his children would have both, and that he would only have children by his wedded wife.

"It's not a problem. I have condoms." She held one up.

He scowled at it through the dimness. "My God." She had actually planned to spend the night with a stranger from Rowdy's Roadhouse, then?

She slipped the condom somewhere back under the blankets and got up even closer, nose to nose with him. "Don't ask, all right? Just accept that I have them, and let's take it from there."

It was too much. The whole day of watching her, remembering and trying so hard *not* to remember, yearning and telling himself he didn't burn. Chasing her down when she tried to get away from him. And then being forced to watch her some more while she danced with one cowboy after another. Having to take down that fool who had dared to go too far with her.

The drive through the blizzard. The old man in the pickup. The crash.

And most of all, the hours with her pressed up close against him, making him burn for her, bringing all the old memories flooding back so powerfully he couldn't deny them, breaking his lonely, solitary heart all over again.

It was too much.

If she still wanted him for one last time, who was he to deny her?

To deny himself?

To hell with denial. For once. For tonight.

She made a small, hopeful sound.

And what was left of his resistance crumbled to dust.

He took her mouth, hard and deep. She opened for him. He wrapped his arms good and tight around her and he kissed her long and thoroughly, with no holding back.

"Oh, Marcus." She sighed when she lifted her mouth from his.

And then they were fumbling, getting their clothes out of the way without completely undressing, trying to keep the blankets and the tarp close around them as they got their bodies bare enough to touch, to stroke.

To join.

She opened his heavy jacket and pushed up his sweatshirt. She unbuttoned his borrowed jeans and closed her soft fingers around him and he felt he would die right then and be glad to go.

He undid her satin jacket, unhooked her lacy little bra, freeing her breasts to his hungry hands. He pulled up her skirt so it was around her waist. And he tore at her tights until they split down the center seam.

It was awkward and groping.

And he didn't care. Judging by her eager moans and breathless, sweet sighs, she didn't mind, either. They were belly to belly, skin to skin at last, again, after all these years.

She was the same as he remembered her, the same, only better. Her breasts a little fuller, her skin still warm satin under his hands, her scent enough to drive him gloriously mad.

At the last, before he finally claimed her, she brought out the condom and rolled it down over him. He blinked, dazed with need for her.

She gave a low, throaty laugh that seemed to dance

along every one of his nerve endings. "I mean it. Don't ask."

He didn't. He only lifted her on top of him, her legs in their tattered tights folded on either side of his thighs. He gathered the slipping blankets and tarp, tugging them back into place to preserve the wonderful heat they were generating, and he lowered her down onto him. She helped him, sighing, taking him into her by slow, delicious degrees.

Paradise. He had found it again at last. In the middle of a blizzard, stranded in a ditch on a deserted Montana highway. With Rhia.

Because wherever she was, there was paradise.

She rocked him, taking him with her to the edge of the world.

He went where she led him, all the way, surging into her softness, into the sweet, close, wet heat of her body. Too quickly, he felt the end rolling at him, closing over him, opening him up as it hollowed him out. He tried to hold on, for her sake, so she could go over first. He began to fear he couldn't last.

But then he felt her rising, felt the change in her breathing that meant she had caught the wave of her own completion. He knew then that she was close and he set his mind to holding out for her, holding on…

She cried out and stiffened above him, her hands against his chest, pressing at him, as below, she held him within her, hard and tight. He felt her inner muscles closing on him, the contractions of her climax gripping him, easing, gripping again.

It was too good. He couldn't take it. He was going over and there was no stopping it now.

He surged up hard into her and…something opened. Something gave way and suddenly he was feeling her even more acutely than before. It was perfect. A sensation like no other, as though he had found the secret woman's heart of her, as though he touched her, *knew* her in the deepest, most elemental way. He clasped her hips in his two hands and he let his own climax roar through him, turning him inside out as she whispered his name and he pulled her body down to him and claimed her soft mouth in a long, soul-deep kiss.

There was a time after that, the best kind of time. She rested against him, soft and lazy. He stroked her hair and kissed her forehead and wished those sweet after-moments never had to end.

Dawn came as they lay there, not talking, easy with each other in a way they hadn't been since Los Angeles, since their little room at La Casa de la Luna.

She was the one who finally said it. "I think the storm is over." He made a low noise of reluctant agreement. She kissed the side of his neck. "I suppose I'll have to let you up. We'll have to pull ourselves together and return to the real world."

They shared one more kiss. A long one, achingly sweet.

He didn't want to let her go. But of course, he had to. He clasped her hips and gently eased her away from him.

They both looked down at the same time and saw the condom. He was still wearing it, more or less.

It had ripped wide open.


Rhia hated the silence between them.

It was back, with a vengeance, as soon as they saw that the condom had broken.

Not much later, as she was struggling with her ruined tights, buttoning up her jacket and trying to smooth her tangled hair, Marcus leaned over the front seat and opened the glove compartment. He found a pen and a scrap of paper, on which he quickly scrawled a series of numbers.

"Here." His breath fogged on the frozen air.

She took it. "What's this?"

"My cell number. Don't worry, I use an excellent encryption program. No one will know if you call me."

For a moment, she actually thought that she'd read the silence all wrong. That he'd reconsidered and wanted to see her again. Her silly heart tried to leap.

But then she understood. "Oh, seriously. There's nothing to worry about. I'm not pregnant. The timing's wrong—plus, you're being ridiculous. If I were to call you, whatever the reason, I wouldn't care who knew."

"You *should* care. It's not fitting."

She opened her mouth to argue—and then shut it without a word. Arguing with him on that subject would get her nowhere. True, he had just taken her to heaven in the backseat of a freezing SUV. But that didn't matter. The barriers between them hadn't changed. Those barriers were unbreachable, even if they *were* all in his head.

She stuck the scrap of paper in the pocket of her jacket, with her permit and the electronic key and the one unused condom. "All right. What next?"

"We get out of here and up to the road and see if we can flag down a passing motorist."

The rear door of the SUV opened easily. They went out that way. Marcus insisted on putting her over his shoulder and carrying her up the side of the ditch through new snow that reached almost to his knees.

At the top, by the roadside, he gently let her down. "Are you all right?"

"Perfect." She aimed her chin high and gave him a regal smile. Yes, she did know that she wasn't a pretty sight. But except for her poor, cold feet in her soggy, stained Manolos, at least she was warm. She wore the blankets for a coat, glad that they covered her to her ankles as she'd had to remove her tattered tights, which she'd tucked into the front of her skirt when he insisted she not leave them behind in the wrecked SUV where anyone might find them.

He'd kept the torn condom and its wrapper, slipping the evidence of their indiscretion into a pocket for disposal later. Heaven forbid that someone might find proof of what they'd done together during the long, freezing night.

Marcus's phone still wasn't working. He lit more flares and they waited. It didn't take long. Within five minutes, a snowplow appeared, clearing the drifts of new snow from the highway. Following the plow was a highway patrol car.

The patrolman pulled over and stopped. He'd been looking for them since before dawn, he said. He put them both in his patrol car where the heater was going strong, and he had a Thermos of hot coffee for them. He called his station on the car radio and reported that he had found the princess and her bodyguard and both were uninjured.

They told the officer about the accident and described the old man and his brown pickup.

The officer shook his head. "I would bet my new quad cab that was Loudon Troutdale you almost got killed by."

"You know him?" Rhia asked, surprised.

"Your Highness, everyone in these parts knows Loudon. He's got some kind of record in the county for reckless driving. I'm thinking he's had his license for about a week now after the last big suspension."

Marcus said, "Last night, after the accident, I got out of the car and walked along the road looking for a sign of him. Judging by his tracks in the snow, he managed to regain control of his pickup and continue on his way."

"Can't tell you I'm surprised," the patrolman said. "Loudon always ends up in one piece. The people he runs into are generally not so lucky."

Rhia asked, "Do you think he'll lose his license this time?"

"That'll be up to the judge, but I can't say as how it would be a bad thing if Loudon never got behind the wheel of a vehicle again."

They returned to town. Marcus rode in front with the officer, as was proper—because Marcus was all about what was proper, what was *fitting*.

Rhia sat in back behind the security grate and tried not to feel like a very bad girl. She probably shouldn't have seduced Marcus there at the end after putting the poor man through hell the day and evening before.

To have sex with him on top of everything else? Well, it wasn't very nice. And it was foolish. Worse than foolish. He had said it himself: it was wrong. But she had kept pushing him, whispering to him, teasing him, until he gave in.

Because she still had that *thing* for him. There was just something about him that called to her, something that made her wish there still might be hope for the two of them somehow. Deep in her heart, she feared she would never get over him.

And yet, she had honestly meant what she said to him, that she knew it was finished between them. Their sad, lost love was never going to be resurrected. She accepted that. She'd had no expectations concerning Marcus for six years, not since their encounter in the South of France, in front of that deserted farmhouse that belonged to some distant relative of her mother's. Not since she had cried her eyes out right in front of him, throwing away every last scrap of her pride and her dignity, begging him to give them one more chance.

And he had just stood there, watching her, letting her

thoroughly humiliate herself. Before calmly and irrevocably sending her away.

So, yes. It had been rather a bad idea to have sex with him again.

A bad idea that had turned out absolutely perfect.

Something beautiful and real and honest in the middle of a terrible mess.

She probably *should* regret it. But she didn't.

Instead, she felt, at last, that she and Marcus had reached a certain peace with each other. That something good really had come of that horrible day and night. She felt she could let him go now without resenting him, without the bitterness that had clung to her heart for way too many years.

Yes. All in all, miraculously, it had been a good thing.

Well, except for the condom breaking. That was a bit worrisome.

But the time of the month was wrong. And they had only made love once. That she might become pregnant was very unlikely. Very.

In fact, she was certain that she wasn't pregnant. There was no need to worry on that score. She'd behaved badly, but she did have a lovely, wicked memory to cherish. Every once in a while even the most unimpeachable of princesses had to get out and misbehave a bit.

She had done just that and survived. And now, life would go on.

Rhia felt downright philosophical about the whole experience.

Or at least, she did until the next time her period was due.

## Chapter Six

*Two months later*

"Just take the test," Allie pleaded. "Just get it over with so that you can move on."

"So that I can move on," Rhia parroted wearily. It was a balmy June afternoon in Montedoro. She sat across from her sister on the stone terrace off the living room of her villa. Sipping Perrier with lime, they gazed out over the Mediterranean. "As though taking the test will make everything all right."

"I didn't say that."

"What then? Are you saying you think I'm *not* pregnant?"

"Er, well…"

"Just answer the question."

"I'm saying I think you have to find out either way, so that you can decide what to do next."

Rhia sipped her Perrier. "Tell me. Where, exactly, did you buy those condoms?"

Allie winced. "In the ladies' at that little bar in Elk Creek called Charlie's Place."

"When did you have time to go there?"

"I, um, went in just to have a look, after I rented the red pickup."

"And decided to buy condoms?"

"Because I was hoping to convince you that we might, you know, get a little wild that night to help you forget your troubles. And I went into the ladies' and saw the condom machine and I thought, well, if we're going to be wild, we should be responsible about it."

Rhia watched a sailboat gliding smoothly on the wind-ruffled, turquoise-blue water of the harbor and softly advised, "I would not depend on the condoms from the ladies' at Charlie's Place again."

Allie made a sad little sound. "Oh, Rhia. I'm so sorry. I know this is all my fault and I'm…I'm just *so* sorry."

Rhia relented. "Oh, of course it's not your fault. I didn't *have* to run off to Rowdy's Roadhouse. And I certainly wasn't forced to seduce poor Marcus just because we ended up stranded overnight in a wrecked SUV in a Montana blizzard and I happened to have a couple of condoms."

Allie reached across and squeezed her arm. "You're a darling not to blame me. But I do see my part in what happened. And I'm turning over a whole new leaf, I promise. In the future, I'm giving up all my wild and ill-considered schemes."

"Oh, please, Allie. Your wild, ill-considered schemes are part of your charm. And everything I did that night, I did by my own choice."

"Still, I feel terrible…"

"Well, stop. Sometimes things just happen. You get in

an accident and the condom breaks. You pick up the pieces and you go on."

Allie squeezed her arm again. "Just take the test. Please. You'll feel better once you know."

The next morning, Rhia took the test.

The result should not have surprised her. After all, her breasts had become extra sensitive in the past few weeks and already that very morning she'd had to eat five soda crackers to settle her stomach. Also of late, just the smell of coffee or asparagus had her feeling queasy. She'd always heard that pregnant women developed sudden, strange aversions to various foods and beverages they used to enjoy.

No, the results should not have been a surprise. Since the day several weeks before, when her period was due and didn't come, she had known in her heart that she was going to have Marcus's baby.

Still, as she stared down at the result window of the test wand and saw that she actually, factually *was* pregnant, she had the strangest feeling of complete unreality.

She was shocked, after all. Shocked, stunned and very much surprised. Even though she'd already known. Because somewhere deep inside she'd been secretly expecting to find out that she *wasn't* expecting, after all.

That whole day, she walked around in a daze. At 9:00 a.m. as usual, she and her assistant, Leanne Abris, met in Rhia's office at the National Museum complex to go over Rhia's calendar and touch base on the progress of various projects. Leanne took one look at her and asked, "Ma'am, are you ill?" Rhia made some excuse about not sleeping well and they got on with business.

But then later she had a long conference with Claudine Girvan, the museum's brilliant director. They were

planning an upcoming exhibit of the works of the great
Montedoran-born Impressionist painter, Adele Canterone.
Three times during that meeting, Claudine asked in a worried tone if she was feeling all right. Rhia just kept smiling
vaguely and replying, "Of course. Yes. I am fine."

And she *was* fine. In a pregnant sort of way.

Allie came by that night as she'd been doing just about
every night for the past three weeks or so. They shared
dinner on the terrace.

Once Rhia's housekeeper had served the main course
and left them alone, Rhia told her sister that she'd taken
the test. "I'm having a baby."

"Oh, my darling." Allie jumped from her seat—and
then just stood there, her hand at her throat. "What will
you do now?"

Rhia straightened her shoulders and tried on a smile.
"Have this baby. Live my life—only now, I'll be raising
a child."

"Oh, Rhia…" Allie came around the table then, her
arms out. Rhia got up and Allie grabbed her in a hug.

In a whisper, as she held on tight to her sister, Rhia
confessed, "I don't think I even really believe it yet. But
I always did want to have a family, to have children. And
now I will. I'll just be doing it without a husband."

Allie took her by the shoulders and met her eyes. "You
*will* have to marry eventually. We all do." She referred to
the Prince's Marriage Law, which required all the Bravo-
Calabretti princes and princesses to wed by the age of
thirty-three or lose it all—their titles and the large sums
of money and various properties that were their birthright.
The Prince's Marriage Law was controversial. Many believed it wrong, in any circumstance, to set a schedule
for marriage. The law had been abolished in the past. But
then Rhia's grandfather had reinstated it. He had been the

last Calabretti heir and then managed to produce only one child, Rhia and Alice's mother, Adrienne. The Calabretti family had held the throne of Montedoro for centuries. The Prince's Marriage Law made it much less likely that they would lose the throne for lack of a legitimate heir.

Rhia shrugged. "I have seven years left to find the right man *and* keep my titles and property. I don't think I need to borrow any trouble right now. I have more than enough to deal with as it is, thank you."

"Mother and Father—"

"—will support me in my choice. You'll see."

"And Marcus…?"

Rhia chuckled. It wasn't a cheerful sound. "Don't look so worried. Of course I will tell him."

"When?"

"Right away."

At nine the next morning, Marcus entered the locker room from the training yard, dripping sweat and ready to hit the showers. He stripped down and grabbed a towel.

His cell rang. He scooped it off the bench in front of his locker and answered. "Captain Desmarais."

"Hello, Marcus."

*Rhia.* There was only one reason she would be calling him.

His knees went to jelly. He sank to the bench. This couldn't be real.

But it was real. "Marcus, are you still there?"

"Yes. Right here."

"We…need to meet."

"All right."

"Come to my villa. Do you have a pen?"

"Hold on." He shot upright and flung back his locker door. As luck would have it, there was one, way in the back on the upper shelf. He grabbed it. "Go ahead." She rattled off an address in the ultraexclusive harbor resort area of Colline d'Ambre. He had no paper handy, so he dropped back to the bench and wrote the address on his thigh.

"This afternoon?" she asked.

He'd just returned from a security assignment guarding Prince Alexander and didn't expect new orders for a couple of weeks, which meant he had nothing that day that he couldn't reschedule. "What time?"

A silence on her end. "You're making this so easy." She spoke with false brightness. "At the very least, I expected you to demand that the meeting be secret."

Had he misread the meaning of her call? He didn't see how he could have. They had been very clear with each other. But perhaps there was something else she was calling about, something he hadn't considered.

He glanced around the locker room. He was the only one there. It should be safe to come right out and ask her if she was carrying his child. But someone else could enter at any time. It was always safer to be discreet. Besides, at that moment, he couldn't have pushed the words beyond his teeth if his life had depended on it.

He said, with a formality that even he found ridiculous, "I *would* request that we meet in secret—if what's been between us can ultimately be *kept* a secret."

She made an impatient sound. "Well, it can't be for me. But for you? Yes. Absolutely, it can." Defensive. And angry.

He felt his own anger rise. What was she telling him? That she thought he might actually deny his own child—and that she would aid him in that?

He needed…to see her face. This was not a conversation they should be having over the phone. "Just tell me what time."

A careful sigh escaped her. "Four o'clock?"

He stared at the address on his thigh. It was smeared a little from his sweat. The unreality of this hit him all over again. "I'll be there."

"Wonderful." Her tone told him all too clearly that it was anything but. There was a click.

She had hung up.

At four on the dot a servant led him into a large sitting room furnished with excellent taste and a goodly number of fine antiques. A wall of glass doors opened onto a long terrace. The doors were flung wide. A pleasant breeze touched his cheek.

Beyond the central pair of open doors, Rhiannon sat at a small iron table, facing away from him. On the table beside her were two ice-filled glasses and two bottles of sparkling water.

"Thank you, Yvonne," Rhiannon said without turning. "Nothing else right now." The servant gave him a nod and left. "Marcus." Still, Rhiannon didn't turn. "Please." She gestured at the empty chair on the other side of the table.

He went through the doors. The villa was high on one of the hills overlooking the harbor, so that beyond the squat stone pillars that supported the terrace rail, the view was of clear blue sky and the hills across the water. Pleasure craft crammed the wind-ruffled harbor below.

Rhiannon turned her head to him. When her eyes found him, there was a sharp, jabbing sensation in the vicinity of his heart. She was as beautiful as ever, in a summer dress printed with bright flowers. She'd pinned up her seal-brown hair. He thought she looked tired. Her dark eyes gave him nothing.

He didn't know what else to do. So he retreated behind the habits of a lifetime. He'd worn his uniform. Somehow, civilian dress had seemed disrespectful. His visor cap was already tucked beneath his arm. He sketched a bow. "Ma'am."

Her soft mouth tightened. "Don't be absurd. Sit down." He sat. "Just put your hat on the table," she instructed wearily. He put it down. She offered, "Have some Perrier."

"Thank you." He made no move to touch it.

She poured the bubbly water over the ice in her glass and then set the bottle aside, resting her slim hand on the iron lace of the tabletop. "We are ludicrous. You know that. One time. How pitiful. This was not supposed to happen."

If he'd had a shadow of a doubt, he didn't any longer. He felt frozen in place, struck anew with extreme unreality. He attempted, badly, to reassure her. "It will…be all right."

She weighed his words, staring out over the terrace rail again. "Yes. Of course it will. Eventually." A small, strained laugh escaped her. "After my failures with fiancés, I had begun to believe I would never have children. I think that once I get over the shock, though, once I've become accustomed to the whole idea, I will actually be glad." She stopped talking.

He realized he ought to say something, to reassure her, to make it clear that he fully intended to do what had to be done now. "We must speak with Her Sovereign Highness immediately. And with the Prince Consort."

A frown drew her smooth, dark brows together. "Well, of course I will tell my parents. Soon. But I wouldn't say there's any huge rush about it."

He didn't understand. "Of course there's a rush. It's been two months since that night. The longer we put off the wedding, the more the world will talk. I don't want that for the child, growing up with people pointing, whispering, calling him hurtful names. We need to be married immediately—that is, if Her Sovereign Highness doesn't demand my head for this."

"Your head? Please." She looked at him again. "And what are you talking about? We're not getting married. You never wanted to marry me. You were very firm on that. There is no way you suddenly get to do an about-face now."

His ears felt hot. And his heart had set to galloping. This was a nightmare. "You deserve a prince. I know that. But the child is mine or you would not have called me here." *And no child of mine will be born without my name. No child of mine will grow up without his father, without two parents married in the eyes of God and man.* He swallowed. Hard. And spoke with a composure he didn't feel. "Of course, I understand your reluctance. I am so…sorry. But it can't be helped. It's necessary now that we go to the sovereign and somehow get her to see that we have to marry."

Her mouth was a thin line. "No, it most certainly is not necessary. Not in the least."

He gaped at her as a terrible awareness dawned. "Wait. No. You can't. You wouldn't."

She blinked. "Wouldn't what?"

He strove mightily for discipline. For calm. For reason. If ever there was a moment that demanded a clear head, this was it. And his brain felt like mush. Mush on fire. "I… understand that you don't want to marry me. That you've moved on from wanting much of anything to do with me. And of course, there would be more suitable prospects who would jump at the chance to make a lifetime with you. But that is not going to happen now. Not while there is breath in my body. I'm sorry to disappoint you, Rhiannon. Sorry on more levels than you could ever imagine. But I can't allow this. No other man will have my child. Never. My child will know his father. My child will grow up with parents who are married to each other and devoted to his well-being."

She stared at him for several endless seconds. And then she said with slow, careful deliberation, "Marcus. You understand nothing. You never have. I refuse to marry a man who only wants to marry me because I am the mother of his child. And as to those 'prospects' you mention? There are none. I'm not marrying you. I'm not marrying *anyone.* Not now, anyway. Not for years yet."

Of course she would marry him. She would have to now. There was no other way. He asked, just to be absolutely certain, "There is no one else, then?"

She huffed out a breath. "Do you actually believe I'm that reprehensible?"

He stiffened. "No. Reprehensible? Of course not. I never said that."

"That is exactly what you said—not in words, no. But it was clearly implied."

He knew he was in trouble here and he didn't even know why. Flatly, he defended himself. "I did not."

"You asked me if there was someone else."

"Yes, I did. But that doesn't mean I find you reprehensible."

"What else would you find me if you believe that I would have had sex with you while I was involved in a serious relationship with someone else?"

He hadn't thought of it that way. If the truth were known, he was having trouble thinking, period. Ever since he'd answered her call that morning, he'd felt as though he didn't have a brain inside his head. The last thing he could ever do was to marry the woman beside him. And now to marry her was the thing that he somehow, against all odds, must find a way to do.

Valiantly, he tried again. "I only meant, if you had someone…if you knew someone more suitable than I, someone who would marry you and give the child his name. I only meant, I'm sorry, but I cannot allow that to happen."

She picked up her glass, took a slow sip, set it back down. "Oh. Oh, I see. You were thinking I had perhaps planned ahead and cultivated the acquaintance of some random minor prince, or even some lesser aristocrat willing to call another man's child his own for certain… monetary considerations, or simply for the chance to marry up."

He could not sit in that little iron chair for one second longer. Rising abruptly, he went to the stone rail. Staring out over the harbor, his face to the wind, he spoke without turning to her. "Please, Rhia." He was so desperate to get through to her that he used the intimate form of her name, the form he had tried in the past eight years to completely eradicate from his vocabulary. "I did not mean to insult you." He turned and faced her then. "I don't judge you, not in any way. Except that I respect you deeply and…and you know that I care for you, that I always have."

She wrapped her arms around herself then, hunching her slim shoulders in a self-protective way. And for a moment, she closed her eyes. Her black lashes lay like small silk fans against her too-pale cheeks. When she looked at him again, her expression had lost the tension and anger of a moment before. Now she seemed defeated, infinitely sad.

"You're right." She spoke softly. "I want to be angry with you. I want to…take out my frustrations on you. But that's not helpful. I'm sorry, too, Marcus. I truly am. I've made a mess of everything. I shouldn't have seduced you that night in Montana."

"Don't blame yourself." The words felt scraped out of him, ragged and raw.

She drew back her shoulders, folded her hands in her lap. "But I *am* to blame."

He told the truth. They could have that at least between them. "I wanted you. I've always wanted you. I think you know that. We both...gave in."

"Because I pushed it."

He held her gaze steadily. "Let it be. Let it go."

After a moment, she nodded. "All right. Yes. I'll let it be. It's only that I..." The words wandered off. She glanced down at her folded hands and then lifted her head again. "At least I've told you. Now you know."

"Yes."

"And you know that I'm not going to marry someone just to give our child a name."

"Not *someone*," he clarified. "Me."

She made a small, pained sound. And then she rose, smoothed the slim skirt of her dress and approached him. They turned and looked out over the harbor together. The breeze brought her scent to him, sweet and exciting as ever. "Oh, Marcus. No. I could never marry you now. I meant what I said that night in Montana. What we had years ago, it's over. Too much has happened. There's been too much pain. We can't go back. Don't you see that it's not possible?"

He watched her profile, so pure and fine. One way or another, he would make her see that there was only one choice here. They were going to be married. It was going to happen. He would *make* it happen. "I don't intend to go back. I only intend to marry the mother of my child."

She did look at him then. The wind blew a few dark strands of hair across her soft mouth. She smoothed them away and tucked them behind her ear. "No."

He turned his body so he faced her fully and he tried

another line of attack. "You can't shame your family this way. The tabloids will have a feeding frenzy."

"I doubt that. They've always been more interested in my brothers than in my sisters and me." A faint smile tried to pull on the downturned corners of her mouth. "Except for Alice, on occasion, when she does something wild."

"You will become 'interesting' and you know it, if you're not married when the world learns of the baby."

She shrugged. "The interest will pass quickly. I'm sixth born—and eighth in line to the throne." His Highness Maximilian was the oldest, the heir, and he already had two children. "I'm an extra princess if ever there was one. And I don't see any shame in my decision. Yes, that this happened is completely my fault. I should have been more careful. I should have backed off that night when you said it was wrong. I should have…left it alone. But I didn't. And now there's a baby coming, a baby who will have my love and my complete devotion. And you can still be a father. You just won't be a husband. At least not to me."

He reminded her sternly, "You are a Calabretti, a princess of the blood."

"I am a *Bravo*-Calabretti, thank you very much. We marry for love. And *only* for love."

"Well, all right, then. I love you. I've always loved you."

She stared at him for a very long time. "I could slap your face for that," she said at last.

He reached out and clasped her smooth, bare arms. Heat seared him, just to have his hands on her again. "Do it, then. Only marry me."

Her eyes were dark fire. "No."

He went all the way with it, pulling her to him, lowering his head, claiming those sweet red lips. She gasped. And for a moment, her body went pliant and her mouth was so soft. A sigh escaped her. The past rose up, the days of their happiness. Fifty-eight days of joy and light, all those years ago. In another country an ocean and a continent away....

But then she stiffened again, whipped her hands up between them and shoved at his chest. "Don't. Stop it."

He released her.

She staggered back, her hand against her mouth. "You have to stop this, Marcus. It's too late for us. You know that it is."

He refused to believe that. "You're wrong. It's not too late. Whatever it takes, we are going to marry. I know what it is to grow up a bastard, unwanted. Unclaimed. That is not going to happen to any child of mine."

"The situation is in no way the same. Oh, Marcus, I know it was difficult for you, growing up. But things were different then."

"Not different enough."

She looked at him pleadingly now. "How many ways can I tell you? This baby will be wanted and loved. This baby will have everything. I will make sure of it. You have to see that. Please. Open your mind just a little, won't you?"

He fisted his hands at his sides to keep from grabbing her again—grabbing her and shaking her until she came to her senses at last. "How blind you are. How proud and thoughtless. You're a Bravo-Calabretti. You were nursed at your mother's breast and your father doted on you and on all of your brothers and sisters. You always had what every child needs. You took it for granted. *You're* the one who doesn't understand."

She gasped as if he'd struck her. And then she took another step back and tipped her chin high. "I think we're at an impasse here. I don't know what else to say to you to make you see."

He refused to give up. He would never give up. "I'll tell you what to say. Say yes. Say you'll marry me."

She made a low sound, impatient and regal. And then she went on as if he hadn't spoken. "I know this has been a terrible shock to you and I'm so sorry to have to put you through this—to put you through what will come, to make you a father when you never asked for that."

"Marry me."

She swallowed. Hard. "I want you to know that I will stick by you. I will make certain there is no...penalty for you with the guard or the CCU because of what's happened. And I hope that, in time, we will reach some kind of peace with each other, that we will find some way to work together, as parents, for the sake of our child."

He dared a step toward her. "The way for us to work together is as man and wife."

She put up a hand. "Don't. Do not come one step closer. I mean it, Marcus. You make a mockery of all we once had."

"That is not my intention. You know that it's not. I only want—"

She didn't even let him finish. "Please. I would like you to leave now."

He almost said no, that they had to come to an agreement, now, tonight, that there was no time to waste.

But he'd already said that. And she'd simply refused him.

He was a soldier, after all. He knew all too well that there actually *were* times when discretion was the better part of valor.

He needed to...clear his head. To think it through. He had no power. She was his princess and he was sworn only to serve her. She held all the cards. If she simply kept refusing him, what could he do?

But then he thought of the innocent child they had

made. And he knew he would do whatever it took. Whatever he *had* to do.

"Please," she said again, her voice so soft, full of hurt that they were doing this to each other. Again. "Go."

"Fair enough." With a last bow, he left her, pausing only to grab his hat from the table as he strode by it.

Rhia stayed rooted in place on the terrace until she heard the front door close.

The sound set her off at a run for her bedroom suite. She made it into the bathroom and to the toilet just in time to flip up the seat and drop to her knees.

Everything came up. It wasn't a lot, since her lunch had been very light. But still. It was awful.

And after it was over, she just sat there for a while. She didn't have the energy to get up—which was fine. She still had that queasy feeling, which meant she would probably only end up on her knees again, anyway.

His words kept playing through her head. *"I love you. I've always loved you...."* The exact words she had so longed to hear him say on the steps of that deserted farmhouse six years ago.

How dare he say them now? Her heart raced in sick fury at the very idea.

Which had her bending close to the bowl all over again.

"Ma'am?" It was Yvonne, her housekeeper, hovering in the doorway to the bedroom, her voice low with worry. "What can I do?"

"Some crackers. A glass of water..."

Yvonne helped her up a few minutes later. She led her to the bedroom and made her comfortable in her favorite slipper chair, with the glass of water and the plate of plain crackers on the small table beside her. Then she knelt and helped Rhia off with her sandals.

"Thank you," Rhia said. "Have Elda prepare me a tray. Something light, in an hour or so?"

"I will, ma'am. Anything else for now?"

Rhia shook her head. "No. That will do."

An hour later, when Yvonne brought in the tray, Rhia was able to eat most of her meal. She went to bed early but didn't sleep well.

She kept thinking about that look on Marcus's face when he left her. A look of purest determination.

The irony of the situation did not escape her. Marcus seemed as single-mindedly set on marrying her now as he'd once been determined never to speak to her again. She knew she hadn't heard the last of this from him.

She considered making the first move, calling him again, asking him if they might talk it over a little more in the hopes that they would manage to come to some sort of understanding between them. But she didn't really see how more talking was going to do either of them any good. Not until she had a new approach to the problem. Not until she felt she had a way to make him see what a bad choice it would be, to marry only because there was a child on the way.

Marcus had always been so determined to do the right thing as he saw it. He had no idea what went into a real marriage, had never seen one up close. The fact of the marriage itself seemed the main thing to him, that their child have married parents. He didn't know there could be so much more. He didn't understand that she wanted a chance at a *real* marriage, at a true partnership.

If she couldn't have that, she wasn't sure she could ever bring herself to marry at all—well, not at this point in her life, anyway. She supposed in a few years, when the specter of the marriage law loomed, she might change her tune.

Time would tell about that. What she did know was

that she wasn't marrying Marcus just because there was a baby coming. She had loved him too much once to settle for less than real, true love now.

## Chapter Seven

Rhia went to Alice's villa that night and told her sister everything. Allie was wonderful. She hugged Rhia good and tight and told her what she needed to hear: that everything would work out fine.

Sunday was Father's Day. Rhia went to the palace for dinner with her family in the sovereign's private apartment. She gave her father a small oil painting by one of his favorite Texas artists. He thanked her with a hug and a warm, approving smile. Her father had always made her feel loved and appreciated—which for some reason brought Marcus's cruel words of the other day to mind. He had said that she was blind and proud and thoughtless. That her parents doted on her and she took their love for granted.

Her father tipped her chin up. "Is there something the matter, sweetheart?"

She looked into his eyes and thought how handsome and good he was. She was almost tempted to tell him about the baby right then. But no. The family celebration of her father's special day was hardly the time to go into all that. So she only answered, "Just a little…wistful, I guess."

He chuckled. "Wistful. It's a word that might mean just about anything."

"Thoughtful. Pensive. Will those do?"

"Do you want to talk about it?"

She shook her head. "Happy Father's Day. I love you."

"And I love you."

"You're my favorite father in the whole world."

"Well, considering I'm the only one you've got, I should certainly hope so."

They went in to eat shortly after that. Allie took the chair next to her. "I checked," she teased, leaning close. "No asparagus on the menu."

"Whew. I just might get through this meal without bolting for the loo."

They laughed together.

Overall, it was a lovely evening. Rhia watched her parents fondly—and with more of the wistfulness she'd confessed to her father. Her parents had been married for thirty-six years, yet sometimes they still behaved like newlyweds, sharing tender glances and, at least when it was only the family, touching often.

Her brother Rule and his wife, Sydney, were the same. When they looked at each other, it was obvious to everyone that they were in perfect accord. Max had been like that with his wife, Sophia. Now, three years after Sophia's death in a water-skiing accident, Max still seemed at loose ends without her. He had that faraway look in his eye, as though he'd lost what mattered most and didn't know how to get along without it. Alex and his wife, Lili, and their twins were in Lili's country, Alagonia, that night. But they were every bit as well matched and happy with each other as the other married members of Rhia's family. The Montana newlyweds, Belle and Preston, were the same.

No. Rhia wouldn't settle for less than what her parents and brothers and sister had found. She refused to settle for less. Did that really make her blind and proud and thoughtless?

Allie leaned close again. "You have that look. You know it, right?"

"Look? What look?"

"Stricken, sad and torn apart. Mother and Father are watching you."

"I'm just not ready to tell them about it yet."

"Then perk up and pretend you're having a good time."

Monday came. Rhia dragged herself to the museum to work. Tuesday was the same. And Wednesday, as well.

She kept expecting to hear from Marcus. After all, he'd made it painfully clear that he did not accept her refusal to marry him. She dreaded their next meeting at the same time as she wished they might somehow get it over with.

But he didn't call or try to get in touch with her.

She told herself that was good thing. Maybe he was reconsidering. Maybe he was learning to accept that a marriage between them was not going to happen.

By Thursday, after thinking the situation through from every angle, Marcus was deeply discouraged. He prided himself on being resourceful and focused and capable of strategizing effectively to accomplish any given goal. But every time he tried to plan how to get Rhia to see the grievous error in her decision not to marry him, he came up short.

He had known the truth the other night, when she told him about the baby and then flatly refused his offer of marriage: she had the power. He didn't. She had the wealth and the position and she simply didn't care if the tabloids said hateful things about her. She wouldn't listen to reason and she had no point of weakness he might exploit in order to further his suit.

The situation was dire.

And his powerlessness wore on him. It brought the truth all the more sharply home. The awful irony was not lost on him. She could refuse him now for all of the very valid reasons he had walked away from her before. She was above him and he had nothing to offer her.

The basic questions dogged him, dragging him down. What kind of man was he, if he wasn't going to find a way to claim his own child? If he couldn't make certain that his child didn't grow up a bastard like his father before him?

The answer to those questions was simple and clear. If he couldn't claim his child, he was not a man at all.

Finally, by that Thursday morning, he was desperate enough to accept that he needed input. He needed someone he could trust to help him find the solution that had so far eluded him.

He went to visit his old mentor, the former captain of the Sovereign's Guard, Sir Hector Anteros. Sir Hector, barrel-chested and gray-haired, owned a small house on a quiet cobbled street not far from the shops and open market of the Rue St. Georges. Sir Hector was an old bachelor, recently retired. But the members of the guard and even His Highness Alexander still consulted him on matters that concerned the safety and security of the princely family and of the country itself.

Hector ushered Marcus into his tiny living room and served him bad espresso. Then he sat in his big, tattered easy chair, his feet propped on a faded ottoman, sipping, and said not a word while Marcus confessed that he'd had sex with a member of the princely family entrusted to his care—and gotten Her Highness pregnant in the process.

"Is that everything?" Hector asked when Marcus was done.

Marcus decided that the secrets of the past didn't bear digging up right then. "Everything you need to know, yes."

Hector grunted. "Everything you're willing to tell me, you mean."

"Yes. That's right."

"You should probably be drummed out of the guard *and* the CCU."

"I realize that."

"Followed by disembowelment and a nice drawing and quartering."

"I agree," Marcus bleakly replied. "But that's not why I came to you."

"What is your intention?"

"To marry her. No child of mine will grow up without my name, without the clear and certain knowledge that I claimed him in the way that matters most."

"Did you propose to her?"

"I did. She won't have me."

Hector found that amusing, apparently. He chuckled and sipped from his demitasse. "Why should she? What do you have to offer her?"

"That's the problem. Nothing but my willingness to be a husband to her and a father to the child. And my name. Such as it is." There'd been no indication of what his birth name might be when he was discovered as a newborn on the steps of the Cathedral of Our Lady of Sorrows. So he'd been named Marcus after the priest who found him and Desmarais for one of the wealthy men who endowed St. Stephen's Orphanage. The nuns told him that the couple who adopted him had called him by their last name, but when they gave him up, his name was changed back to Desmarais.

"But Her Highness is having none of you, eh?" Hector's eyes twinkled merrily.

"Are you going to help me or not?"

"Perhaps you ought to try courting her, showering her with flowers and expensive chocolates, with poetry and romantic evenings *à deux*. You ought to put your mind to convincing her of your love and undying devotion."

"I told her I love her. It didn't go over well. I'm no Romeo. You know that. And so does she."

"Then what you need is mercy, my son. The mercy of Her Sovereign Highness and Prince Evan."

The light dawned. "Rhiannon cares about their good opinion. She will listen to them...."

"If you still have your head by the time that they summon her." There was more chuckling.

"You're enjoying this far too much, old man."

"The older I get, the more life amuses me. I have some hope that you will be allowed to keep that head of yours. After all, from the beginning, ever since you were a scrubby little urchin at St. Stephen's, Her Sovereign Highness has had a soft spot for you and your burning desire to grow up and be a soldier for your country."

"That's good, isn't it? That Her Sovereign Highness has kept me in good regard. That could work in my favor."

Hector made a humphing sound. "I will contact the princess's palace secretary on your behalf and arrange an audience for you."

"It must be soon. And if you could arrange for it to be a *private* audience..."

Hector waved a beefy hand. "You're hardly in a position to be making demands."

"They're not demands. They are...urgent requests."

* * *

The following Monday, Marcus received a call from HSH Adrienne's secretary. He was summoned to a private audience with the sovereign the next day at ten-fifteen in the morning. Somehow, Hector had managed to get him exactly what he'd asked for—and damn swiftly, too.

He went to see his mentor a second time to thank him.

Hector gave him more bitter espresso and ribbed him mercilessly about the likelihood that he would end up separated from his head. Marcus tried to take heart from the teasing. He told himself that Hector would hardly be so gleeful over the situation if he believed that Marcus's position was truly dire.

Then again, death wasn't the only penalty that could be considered dire. He could keep his head, but be thrown out of the guard and the CCU, thus losing everything he'd worked his whole life to gain. He could keep his head and be sent away in disgrace. There were any number of punishments short of actual death that he might be sentenced to endure. And how would he claim Rhiannon as his bride, how would he give his child his name, if he lost everything and was banished from his homeland?

In his heart, he believed he deserved whatever he got. At the same time, he knew he would crawl through hot coals naked on his hands and knees if he could only find a way to marry Rhiannon and claim his child.

Wearing his best dress uniform, his mouth as dry as the Sahara at midday, his belly in a thousand knots, Marcus was waiting in the luxurious anteroom to the sovereign's office at 10:00 a.m. At ten-fifteen on the nose, Her Highness's secretary ushered him through the gilded doors to HSH Adrienne's private office.

The sovereign sat behind her giant, heavily carved antique desk at the other end of the large, magnificently appointed room. The secretary announced him.

HSH Adrienne glanced up with a warm smile. She wore a simple white dress with short sleeves and she was, as always, stunningly beautiful. With those mysterious black eyes that seemed to know all and high, proud cheekbones and a wide, full mouth that would have made a movie star proud. She was in her mid-fifties, but looked so much younger—or maybe not younger. Ageless. A goddess of a woman. The most beautiful in all the world. Or so he'd always believed.

Until he met Rhiannon.

His throat locked up at the sight of her. And he was eight years old again and she was wearing a dress of Christmas red, smiling down at him so kindly, calling him by his given name, asking him how he was doing and if he still planned to grow up and join the Sovereign's Guard.

*"Oh, yes, Your Highness. I want to be a soldier. I want to guard you always and to keep you safe."*

*Her smile grew even warmer, if that was possible. "Well, we shall just have to see about that, won't we, Marcus?"*

*"Oh, yes, please, ma'am."*

*"You must be a very good boy and work hard at your studies and do what the sisters tell you to do."*

*"I will, ma'am. I vow it."*

*And then the most wonderful thing happened. So lightly, her smooth, slim hand settled on the top of his head. His heart felt as though it might explode in his chest.*

*A moment later, she took her hand away and moved on.*

Now, all these years later, she spoke as kindly to him as she had when he was eight. "Captain Desmarais, how lovely to see you. You are looking well."

He didn't feel especially well. His stomach gushed acid

and his pulse thundered in his ears. He remained where the secretary had left him, near the door. Too late, he remembered to salute. "Your Sovereign Highness. Thank you."

She rose from her enormous carved chair with its lush red velvet back. "Come in. Let's sit down."

She gestured at a grouping of fine antique wing chairs and a long velvet sofa near the side wall. And then she went over there.

He realized she intended for him to sit down with her. Yes. All right. He could do that.

Stiffly, he approached. He waited until she had perched on the sofa and indicated one of the wing chairs. "Have a chair."

His hat under his arm, he went over there, slid in front of the chair and made himself sit in it, though the last thing he'd ever thought he would allow himself to do was to sit in the presence of his sovereign. "Thank you."

"What can I do for you, Captain? Sir Hector Anteros did tell me it was a matter of importance."

"Ma'am, I…" The words ran out. He had a careful speech planned and agonizingly memorized. But every last word of it had fled his panicked brain.

She tipped her head and studied him. Even in his desperate and determined misery, he knew it for a kind and gentle regard. "Please. Do speak frankly."

His throat had locked up. He had to cough into his hand to clear it. And then, somehow, he managed to ask, "Ma'am, if I might stand?"

She nodded. "Of course. If you wish."

He shot to his feet, locked his knees and snapped ramrod-straight. "Thank you, ma'am."

She nodded again. And she waited.

For a moment, he knew absolutely that he wouldn't be able to say what he'd come to say. But then he made himself think of the child. Of what had to be done, no matter the cost to him, no matter that this woman he revered above all would surely revile him, no matter that Rhiannon would likely never forgive him for going behind her back like this over an issue that was rightfully hers to broach to her mother at the time and place of her choosing.

He realized it was better, it was almost bearable, now that he stood at attention. The speech he'd so painstakingly rehearsed returned to him. "Ma'am, it is with great shame and consternation that I come to you today. I have done something unforgivable and been woefully remiss in my duty to our country, to your princely person and the princely family."

HRH Adrienne blinked. She appeared somewhat alarmed. "My goodness. Certainly it can't be as bad as all that."

"Oh, ma'am. It is. I have…that is, two months ago, when I was assigned as security to Her Highness Rhiannon for the wedding and wedding party of Her Highness Arabella…two months ago, when we were, er, stranded overnight together, we, er…" The words flew away again. He was making a complete balls-up of this interview and he knew it all too well.

Gently, she suggested, "Marcus. Whatever it is, I suggest you simply tell me."

So he did. "Ma'am, Her Highness Rhiannon is going to have my child."

The silence that followed was deafening. Marcus remained at attention, staring straight ahead as HSH Adrienne put her hands to her mouth and then rose and walked away toward her desk again, out of his line of sight. He didn't turn to her. How could he? He doubted he would ever dare to face her again.

She asked from way over there behind him, in a low, controlled tone, "Is that all, then?"

It wasn't. He knew he had to say the rest. And somehow, he did. He spoke to the landscape painting above the sofa. "I want only to claim my own child. But after she told me there would be a child and I proposed marriage, Her Highness Rhiannon then refused me. She insists she will have the child on her own."

"My daughter told you she would deny you paternity?"

He hastened to explain. "No. No, of course she would never do that. She freely admits I'm the father. She simply won't marry me."

"I see," said the carefully controlled voice behind him.

He dared to continue. "I realize that I am in no way worthy of her. And I will willingly bow to any punishment Your Sovereign Highness sees fit to inflict upon me. All I ask is that somehow you find it your heart to allow me to do the right thing by the child and marry your daughter." He paused, but the princess said nothing. So he confessed, "You...know of my history."

"Yes, I do," she said quietly.

"Then please, ma'am, do not allow the same thing to happen to this innocent child. Help me to convince your daughter that she must marry me and allow me to be a true father to our child."

There was another terrible, interminable silence. Then at last, he heard her quiet footsteps again. She reappeared in his side vision, returned to the sofa and sat. "You have come to me, then, without my daughter's knowledge."

He wanted to hang his head, but years of military training did not permit that. "Yes, ma'am."

Did she almost smile? Surely not. "Marcus. Sit down."

He sat.

"Do you love my daughter?"

His sense of complete unreality, so overwhelming since he had entered this room, increased. Love. What an impossible conversation. He sat opposite his monarch whom he revered above all and she was asking him about love. What did he know of such things? "I am only a soldier, ma'am. I only want to do what's right."

She seemed to consider. But consider what? The things he had just said? Her next words? He had no idea. "I understand that for you the legitimacy of your child is of paramount importance."

"It is everything," he said too abruptly. And then remembered to add, "Ma'am." And then he couldn't shut up. "He must know, that I claim him. He must know that I am proud to…own him."

Her Highness swallowed and glanced away before drawing herself up and facing him again. "But for Rhiannon, the situation is not the same. You must see that. From her point of view, the child will not suffer merely because she hasn't married you."

"Not true. He *will* suffer. He—"

She put up a hand. "Please."

He subsided, shocked at himself that he had presumed to interrupt her. "Ahem. Forgive me, ma'am. Go on."

"I only meant that in this day and age, to be born to unmarried parents is not the terrible hindrance and shame it once was."

"That may be so, but—"

"Hear me out. I know that it was a very difficult life for you, as a child, without either parent to care for you. But this child *will* have two parents. Rhiannon has the means and the heart to raise a child as a single mother and I can see that you intend to be a part of the baby's life. And in this case, there is no throne at stake, no succession to secure, no reason the child *must* be born legitimate."

He couldn't let that stand. "Of course there's a reason. The child himself is the reason. Having a family can make all the difference for a little one. It can protect him from the cruelties of the world until he is old enough to face them on his own."

"I do sympathize," she said. "And I'm sorry, Marcus. But in this situation, coercion is not a tool I'm willing to employ."

His heart sank to his boots. "You won't help me."

"I didn't say that."

Hope rose anew. "You will at least talk with her, then?"

"I doubt that my going to her on your behalf will help you. I know my daughter. She won't think kindly of you when she finds out that you've come to me without her knowledge. Are you certain you've done all in your power to convince her that you love her and truly want to marry her?"

"I told her that I love her." He was careful not to add that she had instantly threatened to slap his face for it. "I... pleaded with her. I reasoned with her. I—" He almost said *I kissed her,* but decided that now was not the moment for speaking of kisses. "I tried everything. Nothing helped. She is adamant that she will not marry me."

One raven-black eyebrow arched. "You're certain she won't change her mind, given time and the proper incentive?"

"What incentive? I've done all I could to convince her."

"Ah. But sometimes one must simply try again."

"It won't help. She's made up her mind against me. Ma'am, will you speak with her? Will you try to make her see that our marriage is the right—the *only*—choice?"

The princess shook her head. "You are so very determined, Marcus. I thought I just explained to you that, for you and Rhiannon, marriage is *not* the only choice."

It was at that moment that he realized Her Sovereign Highness had not spoken of punishment, of what she would do to him for having seduced a daughter of the princely blood. But then again, perhaps she *was* punishing him— by not helping him make Rhiannon marry him. To be denied the right to be a father to his child was just about the worst punishment he could imagine.

And it was the child who would suffer the most.

No. He simply could not give up. He *had* to enlist her aid with this. "Will you speak with Her Highness Rhiannon about this, please, ma'am? It's all that I ask."

"Marcus," she chided, unfailingly gentle. "Have you heard a word that I've said?"

"Yes, ma'am. Every word, ma'am."

"Then you know that I don't believe my getting involved will work in your favor."

He drew in a long breath. "Please, ma'am."

The princess stood. Marcus followed suit automatically. "I must speak with her father," she said. "When the prince consort and I have talked this over, I will be in touch with you."

He dared to meet those knowing dark eyes. And he saw that she had said all she would say for now. The interview was concluded. It would gain him nothing to keep on. "Yes, ma'am. Thank you, ma'am."

With a final salute, he turned and left her.

## Chapter Eight

That evening Rhia dined by herself on the terrace. After the meal had been cleared away, she lingered at the little iron table and stared out over the harbor and tried to ignore the nagging worry about what Marcus might do next.

If he did anything at all.

It had been more than a week—eleven days, to be precise—since she'd told him about the baby. In that time, she'd heard nothing from him.

She was starting to believe that he had simply given up, that he'd decided to accept her refusal to marry him. Should she have been content with that?

Probably. But she wasn't. The thought that he might simply let it go left her feeling sad and desperate and very much alone.

"Ma'am."

"Yes, Yvonne?" Rhia turned in her chair to smile at her housekeeper and saw that her mother was there.

Yvonne said, "Her Sovereign Highness, ma'am."

"Mother." Rhia rose and went to her.

"My darling." Her mother held out her arms.

Rhia went into them, glad for the hug, comforted by the subtle, familiar scent of her mother's perfume. "This is a surprise." She offered a drink.

Her mother shook her head. "No. I simply…well, I was hoping we might talk." She was strangely hesitant. And was that an anxious look Rhia saw in her eyes?

Something was going on. Rhia nodded at Yvonne, who left them, closing the doors to the outer hall behind her.

They sat together on the sofa. Her mother carried a lovely Fendi bag, which she set on the coffee table in front of her.

By then, alarm bells were jangling through Rhia. "What's happened?" She touched her mother's hand.

Adrienne clasped her fingers. "Marcus Desmarais came to see me today."

Rhia gasped and jerked her hand away. "He never."

Her mother nodded. "He did."

Rhia got up, went to the open doors to the terrace and stared out, hardly seeing the splendid view.

Adrienne said, "He told me you were having his child."

"Oh, Good Lord in heaven…."

"He is adamant that he wishes to marry you."

Rhia wanted to grab something breakable and throw it. And she also really, really wanted to throw up. But she wouldn't do either. She refused to. She swallowed hard, sucked in a long breath and drew her shoulders back. "Well, that's not going to happen. Which I made crystal clear to him the day I told him about the baby."

Her mother spoke tenderly. "Rhia. Look at me."

She made herself turn and face her mother's waiting eyes. She saw such love there. And wisdom. And true un-

# Get **2** Books FREE!

## Harlequin® Books,
### publisher of women's fiction,
## presents

### ◆HARLEQUIN®
## SPECIAL EDITION

**FREE BOOKS!** Use the reply card inside to get two free books!

**FREE GIFTS!** You'll also get two exciting surprise gifts, absolutely free!

# GET **2** BOOKS

We'd like to send you two *Harlequin® Special Edition* novels absolutely free. Accepting them puts you under no obligation to purchase any more books.

## HOW TO GET YOUR
## 2 FREE BOOKS AND 2 FREE GIFTS

1. Return the reply card today, and we'll send you two *Harlequin Special Edition* novels, absolutely free! We'll even pay the postage!

2. Accepting free books places you under no obligation to buy anything, ever. Whatever you decide, the free books and gifts are yours to keep, free!

3. We hope that after receiving your free books you'll want to remain a subscriber, but the choice is yours—to continue or cancel, any time at all!

## EXTRA BONUS

**You'll also get two free mystery gifts!**
**(worth about $10)**

® and ™ are trademarks owned and used by the trademark owner and/or its licensee.
© 2011 HARLEQUIN ENTERPRISES LIMITED. Printed in the U.S.A.

# FREE!

Return this card today to get
**2 FREE BOOKS and 2 FREE GIFTS!**

## SPECIAL EDITION

**YES!** Please send me 2 FREE *Harlequin® Special Edition* novels, and 2 FREE mystery gifts as well. I understand I am under no obligation to purchase anything, as explained on the back of this insert.

### 235/335 HDL FVQW

*Please Print*

FIRST NAME

LAST NAME

ADDRESS

APT.#

CITY

STATE/PROV.

ZIP/POSTAL CODE

Visit us at:
www.ReaderService.com

Offer limited to one per household and not applicable to series that subscriber is currently receiving.
**Your Privacy**—The Harlequin® Reader Service is committed to protecting your privacy. Our Privacy Policy is available online at www.ReaderService.com or upon request from the Harlequin Reader Service. We make a portion of our mailing list available to reputable third parties that offer products we believe may interest you. If you prefer that we not exchange your name with third parties, or if you wish to clarify or modify your communication preferences, please visit us at www.ReaderService.com/consumerschoice or write to us at Harlequin Reader Service Preference Service, P.O. Box 9062, Buffalo, NY 14269. Include your complete name and address.

◄ DETACH AND MAIL CARD TODAY! ►

**HARLEQUIN®** READER SERVICE— **Here's how it works:**

Accepting your 2 free books and 2 free mystery gifts (mystery gifts worth approximately $10.00) places you under no obligation to buy anything. You may keep the books and gifts and return the shipping statement marked "cancel". If you do not cancel, about a month later we'll send you 6 additional books and bill you just $4.74 each in the U.S. or $5.24 each in Canada. That is a savings of at least 14% off the cover price. It's quite a bargain! Shipping and handling is just 50¢ per book in the U.S. and 75¢ per book in Canada.* You may cancel at any time, but if you choose to continue, every month we'll send you 6 more books, which you may either purchase at the discount price or return to us and cancel your subscription.

*Terms and prices subject to change without notice. Prices do not include applicable taxes. Sales tax applicable in N.Y. Canadian residents will be charged applicable taxes. Offer not valid in Quebec. All orders are subject to credit approval. Credit or debit balances in a customer's account(s) may be offset by any other outstanding balance owed by or to the customer. Books received may not be as shown. Please allow 4 to 6 weeks for delivery. Offer valid while quantities last.

If offer card is missing, write to: Harlequin Reader Service, P.O. Box 1867, Buffalo, NY 14240-1867 or visit www.ReaderService.com

**BUSINESS REPLY MAIL**
FIRST-CLASS MAIL    PERMIT NO. 717    BUFFALO, NY

POSTAGE WILL BE PAID BY ADDRESSEE

**HARLEQUIN READER SERVICE**
PO BOX 1867
BUFFALO NY 14240-9952

NO POSTAGE
NECESSARY
IF MAILED
IN THE
UNITED STATES

derstanding. Rhia's throat clutched and tears filmed her eyes. She resolutely blinked those tears away. "I'm guessing you've already discussed me with Father."

"Yes. We love you. We respect you. We support your choices."

"It can never work with Marcus and me."

Her mother lifted both hands and then lowered them again and folded them in her lap. "I do understand that you...come from different worlds."

She made a scoffing sound. "You sound like him. I don't care about any of that. It's not what I meant."

Adrienne tipped her dark head to the side. Rhia recognized the movement. Her mother was thinking, putting things together the way she so skillfully could. Sometimes Rhia wondered if her mother could read minds. Adrienne said, "I seem to recall that years ago, there was someone. Someone very special. You never said his name. It happened when you were at UCLA, didn't it? And wasn't Marcus there, too, during your freshman year?"

Was her mother saying that she *knew,* about the affair so long ago? Or was she merely trying to add one and one and come up with two, dangling the hook to see if Rhia would bite?

It didn't matter. It was long over. Done. "I don't want to speak of the past. I truly do not."

"My darling, I only want to point out that you've been engaged twice since then and couldn't make yourself go through with the wedding either time."

"Oh, please. Do we have to do this?"

"He's a fine man. I don't think he has any idea how much he's accomplished from such difficult beginnings, or of how far he could go."

"You think I don't know that? You should tell that to him."

"I'm only saying, why refuse him out of hand? You aren't required to say yes or no right away. You could… make an effort with him, give the two of you a chance to find out if there might be a future for you together, after all."

A headache had begun to pound at her temples. And her stomach still threatened to rebel. "Please don't make me explain it all to you. I can't bear it right now."

"All right." Her mother was silent. She gazed steadily at Rhia, her expression thoughtful. And then she said, "You know that I love you. And so does your father."

"I do know. And I am grateful every day for all you have given me."

"I know you must be livid with Marcus about now, for coming to me about this."

"Livid doesn't even begin to describe it."

"But you could look at it another way."

"Oh, really? What way is that?"

"Think of his courage. His ingrained sense of honor and his absolute desire to do the right thing by you and by the child. Think of what it must have cost him to come to me, his sovereign to whom he's looked up from early childhood, to admit to my face that he had stepped so very far beyond the boundaries of his position, that he had become…intimate with you, my own beloved daughter, when his sworn duty was to see to your safety and well-being. Rhia, I'm certain he expected me to order his arrest."

Rhia sighed. "Yes. Well. I imagine he did expect that."

"And yet he came to me, anyway."

"He's like that."

"You would search long and hard to find another man so worthy. I think you *have* searched. And we both know what you've found."

"Mother. I just don't think there's any way it can work with Marcus and me."

Adrienne picked up her handbag and stood. "But you will give it some thought?"

"Honestly? Right now, it's *all* I think about."

"Good, then. Neither your father nor I can ask for more."

As soon as her mother was out the door, Rhia ran to the bathroom and lost most of her dinner. Once that unpleasantness was finished, she brushed her teeth and threw on a robe and asked Yvonne for hot tea and crackers. The housekeeper brought the bland snack to her bedroom and Rhia thanked her and told her she was free to retire for the night.

The bedroom had its own section of terrace overlooking the harbor. She opened the French doors to let in the sea breeze. She'd just taken a chair and picked up a cracker when the phone rang.

A glance at the display told her it was Marcus, which did not surprise her at all. Her stomach feeling a bit fluttery, but in a whole different way than earlier, she set the cracker down and answered. "Have you called to make your confession, Captain Desmarais?"

He knew right away what she meant. "You've spoken with Her Sovereign Highness, then?"

She tried to drum up a little of the outrage she'd felt before her mother started pointing out all of his sterling qualities. "You went behind my back."

"I'm sorry. I felt I had no choice. And now I find…" His fine, deep voice trailed off. He tried again. "I feel very guilty."

"And well you should."

"Rhia. I know it was wrong, but I had to do what I could to try and get you to reconsider."

"You just called me Rhia again." She felt absurdly gratified.

"Yes." Was that a hint of actual humor she heard in his voice? "Now that we're having a baby, it seems somewhat ridiculous not to use your name."

"It's always seemed ridiculous to me."

"I'm aware of that," he answered wryly. And then, with some urgency, "When can I see you again? When can we talk?"

She should make him wait, after what he'd done. But she couldn't. He was her greatest weakness and he always had been. "Now? Tonight?"

"I'm on my way."

Marcus had raised his hand to ring the bell when the door opened.

She stood before him looking beautiful and exhausted in a blue satin robe. Her gaze tracked over his casual trousers and knit shirt. "It's nice to see you out of uniform."

Anxiety for her well-being had him demanding gruffly, "Are you ill? Is the baby—?"

She waved a hand and commanded softly, "Come in." Stepping back, she gestured him forward.

He entered the stone-floored foyer and she shut the door behind him. "Rhia, are you all right?"

"I'm well. Stop worrying." She retied the sash of the robe and turned to lead him into living room.

He dared to reach out and pull her back. Beneath the smooth satin, her flesh was soft. Warm. And so well remembered. "You look worn out."

She glanced down at his fingers gripping her arm and then back up at him. He probably should have released her. But he didn't. "Marcus," she said finally. "I'm pregnant.

I have morning sickness. Except, well, the morning part? For me, it's more like morning, noon and night."

He didn't like the sound of this. "That can't be normal. Can it?"

She turned into him then and put her hand on his chest, as though to ease his racing heart. It didn't help. His heart only raced faster. "All the tension makes it worse," she said. "But yes, it's normal. I've been to see my doctor and he says I'm fine." Her soft lips were tipped up to him.

He wanted to claim them. It was harder than ever to resist her now that everything had changed, now she carried his child and he knew that he would do whatever he had to do to make her his. "You have to take care of yourself." His voice was rough with desire even to his own ears.

All those years of turning away from her, of denying the power she held over him, of waking from dreams of her and telling himself that dreams meant nothing. Those years were catching up with him now.

The fortress of denial was crumbling, leaving him openly yearning. Leaving him starved for the feel of her flesh pressed to his.

A dimple had tucked itself in at the corner of her beautiful soft mouth. "Marcus."

"What?" He growled the word.

"Are you going to kiss me?"

"What the hell." He took her mouth, hard. At first. She made a small, surrendering sound and tenderness rolled through him in a wave. He gentled the kiss. Jasmine and vanilla and the only woman who ever mattered filled his senses.

It lasted only a moment and then she was pushing him away. He let her go reluctantly, the taste and the scent of her making his head swim and his body burn.

She chided, "We do need to settle a few things, don't you think?"

He drew in a careful, steadying breath. "Absolutely."

She straightened her robe again. "Come into the living room. Please."

The night was balmy. They ended up on the terrace, staring out at the crescent of moon that dangled above the hills across the harbor.

She said, "My mother has urged me to give you a chance."

He sent a grateful prayer to heaven for the goodness and generosity of his sovereign. "Her Highness's wisdom is legendary."

The breeze lifted her shining dark hair, carried the scent of her perfume to him. "Yes, well. I must confess she can be very convincing."

Relief surged through him. "We can be married immediately. Now that it's settled, everything will fall into place."

She was leaning on the railing, staring out at the view. But then she straightened. "Hold on."

*Hold on?* He didn't like the sound of that. "What now?"

She turned to him, drawing her shoulders up the way she did when she prepared for conflict. She even stepped back, claiming distance between them. "I said a *chance.* I didn't say I wanted to race to the altar."

"But you said that Her Highness had convinced you." He kept his tone even and reasonable, though he didn't like the turn this conversation had taken.

She hitched her proud chin higher. "She did. She convinced me that you and I need to spend time with each other, to see if we might find a way to forge a future together."

"Time." He kept his voice level, but it wasn't easy.

Her dark gaze scanned his face. "Marcus. Don't look at me like that."

He pressed his lips together. "Like what?"

"Like you want to grab me and toss me over your shoulder and run for the nearest priest."

It was exactly what he wanted to do. But apparently, she wouldn't allow it to be that simple.

He took a moment to regroup, shoving his hands in his pockets, glancing away toward the moon before facing her again. "How much time were you thinking?"

She looked adorably anxious and she fiddled with the tie of her robe again. "Well, I don't know. I thought we could play it by ear. I thought you could move in here, with me—in separate rooms, of course, at first."

His pride jabbed at him. "Move in with you. Live off you, you mean."

She looked hurt and he instantly despised himself. "Well, um, where did you think we would live?"

He shut his eyes, drew in a slow breath. And confessed the truth. "I didn't think. Except for the necessity that we marry as soon as possible."

"You would want me to come and live with you?" She said it as though it were actually a possibility.

It wasn't. He had a one-bedroom unit with a single bath, in housing provided by the CCU. By his calculation, it would be another three years before he could afford his first house. It would be small and no doubt in need of repair—and certainly not in the luxurious harbor area. "No. No, of course not. You can't live with me, not where I am now. And you wouldn't want to."

"I can't?" She frowned.

"I mean, it's a single officer's unit. We would have to be married first and then I would have to put in for something bigger. And it still wouldn't be…" God. How to say it without sounding pitiable and so far beneath her he wasn't fit to kiss her pretty toes. "It wouldn't be what you're accustomed to."

She moved closer then and she put her soft hand on his chest again. "If we *were* married—which isn't going to happen right this minute—I would be proud to live with you in CCU housing."

There was so much to consider. He hadn't given much thought to any of it in his blind rush to get her to see that they had to marry, and do it quickly. "I don't think CCU housing will be appropriate for you," he said carefully, his body aching for her, his mind and heart once again all too aware of how very far she was above him, of how impossible their marriage was going to be in practice.

Impossible.

But absolutely necessary now.

"Oh, Marcus." With a tender sigh, she moved closer again and let her shining head droop forward on the stem of her neck, resting her forehead against his shoulder. "You're going to have to relax a little, you know? You're going to have to let loose of some of your pride and your hidebound sense of what is fitting."

He cradled the back of her head, eased his yearning fingers into her silky, fragrant hair. And then he whispered only a little raggedly, "Pride and what's fitting have served me well."

She lifted her head. Her eyes beckoned—dreamed of, longed for, never to be.

And yet, here they were. Together. After all these years.

They had made a child.

And somehow, he had to see to it that they *stayed* together, that they married and made some kind of settled life side by side. He had to give his child the essential things he'd never had.

"Less pride," she whispered, her breath so sweet and warm across his throat. "Forget what's fitting."

"I can never forget. Marry me."

She looked at him so tenderly. And shook her head. "We must have time first."

With a low growl of frustration at her stubborn refusal to do what must be done, he dipped his head and captured her lips. Because he *had* to, because the need was growing in him, to taste her again. To make her his.

They had to get married. She might say there was another choice. But for him, there was only one. Even if he could never be equal to her, even if she would forever be the princess he had no right to claim.

She kissed him back, eagerly, opening to him, sucking his tongue into her mouth where it was wet and slick and wonderful. He stroked those silky inner surfaces and pulled her closer, banding his arms good and tight around her.

Too soon, she broke the kiss. "Oh, Marcus…." She stood on tiptoe, pressed her tender lips to the side of his throat. "I mean it. Time." She breathed the words onto his skin.

He stroked her hair. Living silk. "How much time? The longer we wait, the more people will talk."

She chuckled, the sound a little bit sad. "It's not the Middle Ages. You really need to come to grips with that. I meant what I said. I want you to move in here. I want to…try and be close with you in the ways that matter. I want to see if we might have a prayer for a real marriage, you and me."

It wasn't what he'd hoped for. But he supposed it was the best he was going to get at this point. "I would have to keep my quarters. At least for now. Now and then, depending on my duties, I would need to stay there. And as you probably know I often travel, providing security for your sisters or your brothers."

"Yes. Of course. I understand that."

"But when I'm not on assignment, I could be with you here most of the time…."

She let out a happy little cry and clasped his shoulders. "You mean you will?"

He gave her the unvarnished truth. "I will do whatever I have to do to get you to marry me, to give our child my name."

She caught his face between her hands. "Do you have to sound so grim about it?"

He made his lips curl upward. "I shall try to be more cheerful."

"See that you do," she instructed sternly. And she brushed the hair at his temples with the backs of her fingers, the way she used to do all those years ago, when they were secret lovers in California.

He turned his head, kissed the soft pad of flesh at the base of her thumb and then nipped that softness between his teeth, enjoying the small, eager shiver that moved through her and the way her eyes got lazy, the twin fans of her thick, dark eyelashes lowering as she sighed. He couldn't help but wonder: If he took her to bed now, could he get her to give in and marry him right away?

His body responded instantly to that idea.

Her hips were pressed to his. She knew exactly what was going on with him. And she clucked her tongue and shook her head. "I confess, I *am* tempted…." She tipped her head to the side, studying him, and he saw the shadows beneath her eyes.

Seduction would have to wait. He ordered his body to back off and kissed her forehead. "You need a good night's sleep."

"Always so noble," she said with a teasing frown.

"Not as noble as I ought to be. But you have to take better care of yourself, starting with getting your rest."

"Oh, I suppose you have a point. Though making mad, passionate love with you would be so much more fun."

"I will be more than happy to oblige you—once you've had some sleep."

"Oblige me?" She groaned. "This is not how I planned it."

"Planned what?"

"This conversation. I expected you to try to seduce me into saying yes right away."

He shamelessly lied. "I would never do such a thing."

"Yes, you absolutely would. You've already confessed the truth, Marcus."

"What truth?" He tried to look innocent and knew that he failed.

"You'll do anything to get me to marry you."

"Yes, well. You have me there."

"It's all so very ironic, isn't it? You walked away before and wouldn't look back...."

He tried to see the humor in it. "And now you can't get rid of me."

"So I had a pretty good hunch that tonight you would try to seduce me. And then I was going to stand firm and explain how we not only wouldn't be getting married right away, we weren't having sex, either. Not until I felt we were...closer."

"Ah." He bent, nuzzled her ear. "Closer..."

She lifted her arms again and twined them around his neck. "But now, here you are, and I find I only want to... melt into you."

He didn't speak. He didn't dare. And he didn't move,

either. If he did, he would sweep her up in his arms and stride off down the nearest hallway in search of a bed.

She slipped a hand between them and he almost groaned at the thought of what she might be reaching for. But then it turned out to be only the pocket of her robe. She brought out an envelope. "I want you to move in right away. Tomorrow." Taking his hand, she put the envelope in his palm and closed his fingers around it. "Most of the time, Yvonne will be here to let you in. But if she's not, here's the key and the alarm code."

He explained, "I have training exercises in the morning and a couple of briefings. But I can get a few things together and be here in the afternoon...."

"If I'm still at the museum, Yvonne will show you to your room. You must make yourself completely at home." She said it as though she believed it, that he could ever be at home in a house such as this.

Regretfully, he put himself away from her. "Now I should go."

She pressed her lips together and nodded. He turned for the door. "Tomorrow." She said it softly. Almost hungrily. "Promise me."

"I promise," he solemnly vowed. "In the afternoon..."


Rhia called Allie right after Marcus left and explained all the latest developments.

"So he went and talked to Mother," her sister said with a smile in her voice. "The man's got stones, I have to say."

Rhia made a humphing sound. "He really shouldn't have gone behind my back."

"I don't know. I kind of admire a man who does what he has to do to get what he wants."

"That's certainly one way of looking at it."

"It's the *right* way to look at it. And I know you secretly agree with me, no matter that you feel you have to say that you don't—and now he's moving in with you. Good. Excellent, even."

"We'll see."

"Rhia, be bold."

Rhia made a face at the far wall. "Oh, please. What is that supposed to mean?"

"For eight years, you haven't been able to forget that man. Now, at last, the two of you have your chance together. Don't blow it."

"Oh, Allie…" All at once, Rhia's throat felt tight and tears filmed her eyes. "I'm so happy."

"That's more like it."

"And I'm afraid, too. What if we…can't find our way to each other in the end?"

"Don't think like that. You can't afford to think like that. Just concentrate on the two of you, on making it work. And it *will* work. Just watch."

"Oh, Allie. I do hope you're right."

## *Chapter Nine*

When Rhia got home from the museum at six the next afternoon, Marcus was there. Dressed in jeans and a knit shirt, he rose from the sofa in the living room when she entered.

"Rhia." He set down the big coffee-table book he'd been looking at and stood to face her. His shoulders were broader than ever, it seemed to her at that moment. And his eyes…such serious eyes.

They regarded each other. She'd been thinking about him all day, trying to take her sister's advice and think positively. And it had worked, in the main. She'd found herself feeling a rather lovely sense of anticipation for this little experiment in intimacy of theirs.

But now that he was here and she was here and they would have some time to be together that wasn't secret or furtive or only for one night, well, somehow she felt a little awkward. And a lot nervous.

"Is your room all right?" she asked.

"It's beautiful. Very comfortable. Thank you." He studied her face. "You look more rested."

She laughed, a slightly off-kilter sound. "I... Yes. I am. Not long after you left, I climbed into bed and went right to sleep. I slept eight hours straight through. And when I got up, I felt better than I have in weeks. I actually ate a big breakfast. And it even stayed down."

"Good."

"Would you like a drink or a snack? Dinner is usually at seven-thirty...."

"A little whiskey, I suppose."

"Let me get you some." She went to the small wet bar in a corner alcove. "Ice?"

"Neat, thanks." He came closer.

She took the stopper from the crystal decanter and poured him two fingers in a short glass. By then, he was behind her. She turned and handed him the glass.

His fingers brushed hers as he took it and a lovely, hot shiver sang under her skin at the contact. "Thank you." He sipped.

She leaned back against the marble counter of the bar, her hands behind her, gripping the cool rim of smooth stone, and looked up at him. "I feel so...strange. Like this isn't quite real, you know?" He said nothing, only watched her, taking another sip, his eyes going slightly golden, somehow. And she heard herself rambling on, "After all these years, you and me, here in my house. Learning to be together in an everyday way. Sometimes I used to imagine, what it might have been. If you and I had managed to stay together, to make a life together...." Her sentence trailed off. For a moment, there was silence between them.

And then he said, "Marry me."

She shouldn't have, but she thrilled at those two simple words. He moved in closer, set the glass on the counter beside her and then stepped even closer, caging her neatly between his strong arms. More hot shivers cascaded through her.

He said, "If you marry me, you won't have to wonder anymore. We *will* be together. For the rest of our lives."

She felt breathless, mesmerized by the sound of his voice, the gold lights in his green eyes.

He bent closer, captured her lower lip gently between his white teeth, tugged lightly then let go. She let out a quivery sigh. He said, "I talked to your brother His Highness Alexander today."

She *had* to have her hands on him. So she braced them against his chest, which was hard and hot. She could feel the muscular shape of him through his shirt, count the beats of heart under her palm. "About us?"

He nodded. "It only seemed right. He is my commander in the CCU. He needed to know."

"Have you been stripped of your rank? Dishonorably discharged?"

He shook his head. "So far, your family has been amazingly forgiving. However, it's still possible that your father will come after me with a deadly weapon."

She knew better. "That will never happen. My father will always be there if I need him. But he—and my mother, too—are very much about letting their children make their own choices and lead their own lives."

"His Highness Alexander suggests that we marry immediately."

Rhia chuckled, thinking of Alex. Not too long ago Alex and his wife, Lili, had been in a situation very much like the one she found herself in with Marcus now. "Knowing Alex, I'm sure he did more that *suggest* that we marry right away."

"He's right, you know." He bent even closer and nuzzled her hair.

"We need time."

He nipped her earlobe. "You keep saying that."

She let her hands stray up over his big shoulders, along the strong column of his neck, over his nape and into his close-cut hair. "We could make a bargain. I'll stop saying we need time when you stop asking me to marry you."

"I'll never stop." He kissed her temple, her cheek. "Until you stand up beside me and become my wife." And then his mouth was on hers, hot and demanding and so very, very good.

Rhia sighed. He tasted so right. He was everything she'd resigned herself never to have.

And he was pushing her too fast. "Marcus…"

He stepped back instantly. "Too fast?"

She laughed, it was so exactly what she had been thinking. And oh, she did want to grab him and drag him to her bedroom. And maybe she would. In a little while.

But she wasn't going to rush to the altar. No. They did need time, time to fill the same space and find out if they both felt good about being there, time to speak of who they were and where they had been and what they wanted from life.

She touched his arm, letting her hand glide down over the hard, strong shape of it until she reached his hand and could twine her fingers with his. "Let's go for a walk before dinner."

He arched a straight eyebrow. "Trying to distract me from my purpose?"

"Oh, yes, I am. Definitely."

"It won't work, you know."

"Marcus. It's only a walk before dinner. Please?"

* * *

They went down the hill on which her villa was perched and strolled along the pier where all the giant luxury cruise ships were docked. People waved and called greetings to her and looked at Marcus somewhat curiously.

After they'd walked for a while, they got soft drinks from a street vendor and sat on a bench under a tree on the Promenade that rimmed the pier. Rhia sipped the sweet drink and thought how lovely and fizzy it felt, cool and welcoming on her tongue.

Marcus leaned over and tapped his bottle against hers. "You're smiling."

She looked at him and saw her own face reflected in the lenses of his aviator sunglasses. "I always feel free when I walk around Montedoro. You know how it is. We're so security conscious now when we travel outside the principality. But here at home we're still free to move about without trained men watching over us. I hope that never has to change."

He leaned closer. "You don't like having a security detail?"

"It's all right. Necessary, I know that. But it's nicer to be free."

His brow crinkled above the dark glasses. "I've been meaning to apologize...."

She frowned back at him. "Oh, no. What now?"

"I should have asked to be reassigned when I got the orders for the trip to Montana. But I was a coward."

She put her hand over his. "Don't. Please. Yes, I hated it, at the time. But even I understood that refusing your orders wasn't an option."

A muscle in his jaw twitched. "I should have thought of some workable way out."

"Marcus. I swear you have to learn to lighten up a little.

It's water under the bridge…or over the dam. Or however that old expression goes."

"You forgive me, then?"

"Completely. Don't bring it up again."

"Yes, ma'am."

"And don't call me ma'am."

He actually chuckled. And then, for a few lovely minutes, they just sat there, enjoying the shade of the tree, watching the people stroll by on the Promenade. It was quite companionable.

Or it was until two men in the uniform of the Sovereign's Guard came toward them along the Promenade. One was tall and very lean, the other shorter and stocky. They saluted her, murmured solemnly, "Your Highness." Marcus rose.

"Sir," the men said in unison, and saluted him. It seemed to her they made quite a show of it. Marcus returned the salute, but without all the fanfare. Rhia watched the exchange with interest. There was something—challenge, animosity?—in the way the two men looked at Marcus and the way he stared back at them.

The men moved on. Marcus sat beside her again.

She asked, "What was that about?"

"Just two soldiers, men of the guard."

"Do you know them?"

"I do."

"Do they have *names?*"

He let out a slow breath. "Private Second Class Rene DuFere—that's the shorter one. The tall, thin one is Private First Class Denis Pirelle."

"You don't like them?"

He took off his dark glasses, rubbed the bridge of his nose and then hooked the glasses on the collar of his shirt. "I like them fine."

"Marcus," she chided. "What was all that to-do about the way they saluted you?"

"I have no idea. They weren't required to salute, as I am not in uniform. Perhaps they decided going overboard couldn't hurt."

"Hurt what?"

"Rhia, I don't know."

She loosed an exasperated sigh. "Don't you see? This is what I've been talking about. You're always so guarded. Everything is a secret with you."

"It's not a secret. They are noncommissioned officers in the Sovereign's Guard."

"And?"

He glanced heavenward. And then he confessed, "They were at St. Stephen's with me. They are and always have been a…team, you might say. And I never really got along with either of them."

"A team? They're like brothers, you mean?"

He took her hand, held it between both of his and gazed directly into her eyes. "If you have to know…"

"I do. Absolutely."

"We were boys with nothing, no one to claim us," he said quietly, for her ears alone. "Sometimes we formed alliances. Sometimes we made enemies."

"Those two were—are—your enemies?"

He raised her hand toward his lips then. For a moment, she held her breath, sure he would press a kiss to the back of it. But he didn't. She felt regret, but she understood. It was a public place and she was the sovereign's daughter and he just couldn't go that far right then. He said, "We all do what we have to do, to survive."

"You're talking in riddles."

"I don't know how to explain it to you."

"Please. Try."

"You don't understand."

"But I *want* to understand. And I swear to you, Marcus. I would never tell anyone something you told me in confidence."

"I know you wouldn't."

"And I know that there's *something* you don't like about those two men."

"It's not that I don't like them."

"Oh, please. Don't lie to me."

"I swear on my honor. I am not lying to you. We've had our disagreements in the past—Denis, Rene and I—but I don't hold any of that against them now."

"But do *they* hold something against you?"

"I'm sorry. I can't answer for them."

Rhia let it go. She wasn't satisfied with his answers, but it was only their first evening together in this new, more open way. She could hardly expect to know everything in one night. Over on the pier, she saw a man with a camera snapping pictures of them.

Marcus saw it, too. "Now we'll be in the tabloids together."

"Maybe it's only a tourist taking shots for his travel album."

"Do you really believe that?"

"It doesn't matter, Marcus. If we're going to be together, the paparazzi will get pictures of us eventually."

"I don't like it."

She chuckled. "Learn to live with it. You've provided security for most of the members of my family at one time or another. You know how it can get sometimes. Especially if there's any hint of a scandal involved."

He leaned closer and said softly, "All the more reason we should marry immediately." She didn't reply. What was there to say? She'd made herself painfully clear on that subject. He looked at his watch. "It's almost seven. Time we were getting back to the villa, don't you think?"

They were quiet with each other on the walk up the hill.

At the villa, they shared the evening meal, just like a real couple at home alone together, dining in. She gazed across the table at him and remembered what her sister had said.

*Rhia, be bold.*

After dinner, she offered a tour of the villa, upstairs and down. That didn't take long. It wasn't a large house—not compared to the Prince's Palace, where she'd grown up, anyway. The master suite and the living area were on the first floor, with three more bedrooms above and a third floor where Yvonne and the cook had private quarters.

She purposely ended with the master suite. "And this is my room." She led him in there. "My private sitting room…" She led him through the door to the bedroom. "My bedroom." He made an appreciative noise low in his throat and she led him to the next door. "The bathroom." She took his hand and pulled him in there. He flipped on the light. They stood before the wide mirror above the vanity and twin sinks.

"Very nice," he said.

"The tub is big enough for two." She stepped right up to him, put her arms around his neck.

And kissed him.

He captured her face between his two big hands. "Rhia. What are you up to now?"

*Be bold.* "Well, as a matter of fact, I was just about to take you back in the bedroom and show you an intimate view of my bed." It came out slightly breathless. Lord. Was she making a hash-up of this?

But he reassured her—with another searing, perfect kiss. He covered her lips with his and he pulled her closer, so that her breasts flattened deliciously against his hard chest. He even pressed his hand to the small of her back, so she curved into him. He felt wonderful, so hard and strong. He wanted her. She could feel that, too.

Relief and desire swirled through her, making her knees a little weak. She clung to him. He didn't seem to mind.

When he lifted his head, she let her eyelids drift open. He regarded her gravely—or mostly so. There was also a definite flare of heat in his eyes. "I would love an intimate view of your bed."

She touched the side of his face, ran her finger around the neat rim of his ear. "You won't think I have no backbone, will you?"

"Why should I?"

"I said separate beds for a while, remember? That was the plan."

"Plans change." His voice was deliciously gruff. He bent close for another kiss—a sweet, quick, brushing kiss this time.

She stroked the side of his neck, breathed in the clean, manly scent of him. "Allie said I should be bold. And I've decided that I agree with her."

"Bold is good." He feathered another kiss against the tip of her chin and then lifted away a little. "Bold is excellent."

She wrapped her hand around the nape of his neck and drew him closer once more, close enough that they shared the same breath. "Oh, Marcus…"

"Anything."

"Tell me that we will be all right."

"We will," he whispered. "I know we will."

"Tell me we will work it all out."

"We will."

She brushed her lips against his, pressing herself up to him, feeling his heat and hardness, so acutely aware of everything about him: his strength and his goodness. His all-too-ingrained sense of propriety and his natural reserve. His fine, deep voice that made her want to rub herself all over him, the scent of him that had always drawn her. His very pigheaded insistence that she was above him and they couldn't make it work all those years ago.

His insistence that it *would* work—that it *had* to work—now.

"Take me to bed, Marcus."

His answer was to scoop her up high in his arms and turn for the other room.

## Chapter Ten

Marcus reached the side of her high, turned-back bed, and didn't want to put her down. He feared she might change her mind if he let go of her even for a moment—change her mind and send him to the room she had originally assigned him.

She sighed and rested her head against his shoulder. "Um. So…are you just going to stand there holding me all night?"

He bent his head to her. "I might. I might never let you go."

"I might like it, if you never let me go…." She lifted her mouth for him.

He took it, hard and hungrily. She tasted of everything he had ever wanted, all he'd thought he could never have. He sucked her soft upper lip into his mouth, caressed the slick inner surface with his teeth. She moaned. He drank in that sound.

And then, still holding the kiss, he lowered her feet to the floor and began to undress her. She allowed that—more than allowed it. She sighed, swaying against him, whispering "Yes" against his lips as he unbuttoned her silk shirt and eased it off her shoulders, as he unzipped her snug skirt and pushed it down, taking the tiny lace and satin panties she wore along with it. With a flick of a finger, he undid her bra, quickly guiding the straps down her arms, pulling it off, tossing it aside.

She had her hair up. He speared his fingers in it, feeling for pins. "Let it down. Loose." He growled the command against her mouth.

She obeyed, lifting her arms, pulling at the pins until the heavy mass fell in a dark veil to her shoulders. He stroked the seal-brown strands, let the curls fall between his fingers, combing them.

He needed…everything. All of her. To touch her. Every smooth, soft inch.

And he took what he needed. He cupped those fine, full breasts of hers, and he played with her nipples as she bumped her hips against him, sighing, moaning, using her sweet, eager body to beg him for more.

More worked for him. More was exactly what he had in mind.

He pressed his hand against her still-flat belly, wondering at the miracle within, the baby they had made that had changed everything.

"Oh, Marcus. Yes…"

He inched his fingers lower, until he touched the short, silky curls that covered her sex. She lifted to him, moaning more yeses into his mouth.

So he went on touching her, parting her, delving in where she was so wet and sweet and ready for him. He found the hard little nub where her pleasure was centered and gave it special attention.

About then her knees gave way.

She clutched at his shoulders. "Marcus!"

"It's all right. It's good…" He eased her down across the bed, guided her slim legs apart and stepped in close between them. Bending over her, he pressed his mouth to hers.

She kicked away her shoes and caught his wrist to guide his hand. He knew already what she wanted from him. He gave it, caressing her the way she'd always liked it most, so long ago, in California. He dipped one finger in, then a second….

She cried out again. He cupped her, holding her, and let her rock herself against his palm as the finish took her.

A moment later, she went lax. She stared up at him through glazed eyes. He started to step back. She grabbed his arm and held him close and began pulling at his shirt. "Take this off. Now. All of it. Everything…"

Getting everything off sounded like a fine idea to him. He reached both hands back, gathered the shirt up and yanked it over his head. She got hold of it and threw it off the far edge of the bed.

He started to straighten again, so he could take down his jeans.

"Come back here," she insisted, reaching for him.

"One minute. Less."

She let him go long enough for him to kick off his shoes and tear off his socks, to pull his fly wide and shove his jeans down along with his boxers.

"There," she said approvingly. "Better."

He leaned close to her again, sliding a hand under one smooth thigh, lifting that leg, pushing it wider as she gazed steadily up at him, dark eyes full of night and wonder and sex.

"Oh, Marcus. At last. Yes…" She reached down between them.

He groaned at the pure perfect agony of it as she encircled his aching hardness and drew him to her, touching the tip to her wetness, guiding him where she wanted him to be.

He surged forward, filling her.

She cried out. She pushed herself up to him, taking him deeper. He went. All the way, burying himself in her wonderful heat, her unbearable sweetness. He went deep. The moment hung suspended.

The sight of her, below him, open to him, *his* in a way that he'd never allowed himself to think of her before….

That made him drive harder, move deeper within her, withdrawing only to surge close again.

It was glorious. Perfect. He wished it might never, ever end.

But of course, it did. The wave rose up, cresting over them. He went first, turned inside out by it, surging over, flying high.

And then he felt her contracting around him. He braced his arms on the mattress to either side of her flushed, beautiful face and he let her have him, let her move against him at her will. She called his name as she found the absolute hot center of her own pleasure.

She didn't give him long to recover before she was pulling at him again, arranging him to her satisfaction, dragging him fully onto the bed with her, so that they both lay with their heads on the pillows.

"There," she murmured. "Better. Wonderful…"

He nuzzled her hair, cupped one breast, flicking the

hard pink nipple so that she sighed. "You amaze me. You always did. So damnably beautiful…." He stuck out his tongue and licked the perfect, swirling shape of her delicate ear.

She laughed. "I have to ask…"

He nipped her earlobe. "What now?"

"Boxers? When did you start wearing boxers?"

"Boxers shock you?"

"It's just…you always wore briefs before."

"I like boxers. They're comfortable. And what does it matter?"

"It's a little thing," she admitted.

"Exactly."

"But little things do matter, especially now. I intend to know everything about you."

He grunted and thought of the biggest secret, the one he had never planned to tell anyone, the one he supposed he would now have to find a way to tell her. Because she wanted all his secrets and he'd more or less promised he would give her whatever she asked of him.

And he would. Just not right now. He couldn't bear to tell her now.

So he kept it light. "Everything? Be careful what you ask for, you just might get it."

She wrinkled her nose at him. "You've always been much too self-contained. When did you start wearing boxers?"

He smoothed her hair, loving the feel of it under his palm, catching a lock of it and rubbing it between his thumb and fingers. "If you must know, I bought some in a department store, in America, when I was providing security for your sister last fall. I tried them."

"*Silk* boxers?"

"What can I tell you? Silk feels good."

"I don't remember boxers, that night in Montana…."

"It was dark under that tarp, and we were…" He sought the word.

She offered it. "Urgent. It all seemed so urgent."

He remembered. And agreed. "Yes, it did."

She braced up on an elbow and stared down at him through somber eyes. "It was so strange, in Montana at the wedding, to see you shaking hands with the McCade men, and to realize that you had been there, lived in the ranch house there, with Belle and Charlotte…" Her voice trembled a little.

"Shh." He pulled her down to him again, kissed her hair, her cheek, the tip of her nose.

"It's only, well, it hurt. To think that you had been there for months, and I didn't even know."

"Rhia. Why should you know?"

She gave a slight shrug. "You're right." Her voice was thoughtful and more than a little bit sad. "Of course, you're right—but it's strange. When you come right down to it, I know so little of your life. And you know my sister's new husband better than I do."

"Not really. I like Preston McCade. He's a good man. Solid. Dependable. Strong. But we hardly became friends."

"It must be a lonely kind of job, watching over someone for months like that, having to stay close to them constantly, but not really being a part of their lives."

"I never thought of it that way. It's a job that I'm good at. And an honor to be chosen, to be counted on, trusted to protect the ruling family."

She touched his face again. "Lonely, though."

"Yes, I suppose. A little."

"Do you plan to be in security for all of your military career?"

He buried his nose in her hair, loving the scent of it. So sweet. So tempting. "We'll see."

She canted up on her elbow once more and gazed at him with reproof in those soft, dark eyes. "You're being secretive again."

"No. It's only that it's hard to know what opportunities might present themselves." She just went on staring down at him, waiting for more. So he continued, "The Covert Command Unit is a force of only fifty. And the Sovereign's Guard, of which the CCU is part, has two hundred and thirty-three men and women in total. I hope someday to reach the top rank of colonel."

"Would that be so impossible?"

"In such a small force, commissioned officers are few and far between. And as for earning more bars and stars, well, there are the French to consider. By tradition, French officers always claim the highest ranks among us. However, my prospects are even brighter now, with His Highness Alexander so closely involved. And I'm in the CCU, which he created, so that's also a plus in terms of my advancement. His Highness approves of raising up those of us who are Montedoran by birth. But still, we can't all be at the top, can we?"

She laid her hand against his heart. "I think you could achieve just about anything you set out to do."

He looked in her eyes and saw her sincerity. "Marry me."

She came back down to him, resting her head on his chest, where her hand had been. "Time, Marcus. Give us some time."

Rhia thought that things went well between them over the next few days. He left her early in the morning to go to CCU headquarters. But he came home for dinner. They took more walks down by the pier and along the beaches near the casino. And he moved his few toiletries to her bathroom, hung his clothes in her closet.

And every night they shared her bed.

That was wonderful. To spend her nights with him. And not only for the heady magic of their lovemaking. There was so much more. She loved to hear his even breathing beside her as he slept, to wake in the morning with him wrapped around her, so big and warm and strong.

He had always made her feel safe. Cherished. Protected in the purest sense of the word. But now, living openly with him at last, she felt more content and more truly at home than she'd ever felt in her life before.

She only hoped that it could last.

On Saturday, the first story about them appeared in a certain tabloid paper. It included several pictures of the two of them, pictures snapped on the Promenade that first night he'd moved in with her. The headline? *The Princess and the Bodyguard.* As usual with the tabloids, the story was full of trite phrases and heavy on the innuendo. The upshot was that there must be romance in bloom between Her Highness Rhiannon and Captain Marcus Desmarais.

Marcus hated it.

Rhia laughed and reminded him that it was only the truth. "And it doesn't say anything bad about either of us."

"It says that I was a foundling child raised by nuns and that you have been twice engaged and never quite made it to the altar."

"The truth. How terrible." She faked a shiver. "Honestly, we couldn't ask for more."

"Yes, we could. How about if they all learned to mind their own business?"

"Please. That is never going to happen."

He grumbled, "Even if I finally convince you to marry me, those bastards can count."

"Yes, I'm afraid that's true."

"The world will know that you were pregnant *before* the wedding."

"Undoubtedly so."

He tossed the tabloid aside and pulled her close. "Marry me now."

She kissed him. "Give it time, Marcus."

He grumbled something under his breath. But then he pulled her back to him and settled his warm lips on hers again. That led to a much more satisfying activity than arguing over what the tabloids would say.

Sunday, together, they went to breakfast at the palace. It was something of a family tradition. She and her brothers and sisters and their families would join her mother and father in the sovereign's apartments for a private family meal.

That Sunday, the last Sunday in June, Alex and Lili were in Alagonia, and Belle and Preston were in Montana. But everyone else came. Marcus didn't say much through the meal, but her siblings and her mother and father each made a point to engage him in friendly conversation, to show him he was welcome among them.

Rhia knew by the way they all behaved that her parents or Allie or Alex must have told the rest of them exactly what was going on.

Later, when she and Marcus were alone at the villa, he said, "They all know, you realize that? About the baby, and that I'm living here, that I want you to marry me and you haven't said you will."

"Yes. I gathered that everyone was up to speed on our situation."

"Our *situation?*" He repeated the word as if it were an

obscenity. "I'm surprised one of your brothers didn't grab a weapon and run me through."

"As a matter of fact, my brothers respect and like you. You're quite admired in my family, you know."

"Admired, humph."

"Everyone knows you're a good man to have at one's back. They know that you came up from nothing and have done very well for yourself. And that you will forever and always strive to do the right thing."

"They also know that I have no fortune and I seduced their sister."

"Well, *I* have a fortune, so if we do marry, we have that covered. And the seduction, as we both know, was probably more my doing than yours."

"That is not the point."

"Yes, to a great extent, it is."

"The point is that I presumed to have sex with a princess of the blood."

"Yes, but the good news is that you're a commissioned officer, which makes you a gentleman—self-made, but still. They see you as someone dependable who can be counted on to be a good husband and father. And as for having sex with me, well, these things happen."

He paced the living room. "No. No, they don't. Or they shouldn't."

"Marcus, you are such a complete snob. And so annoyingly straitlaced."

He stopped, whirled. Faced her with a lowering frown. "I am not straitlaced."

"No complaints on being called a snob, eh?"

"I didn't know which insult to tackle first."

She stifled a chuckle. "Marcus. You *are* a bit of a moralist, really."

He dropped to a chair as though the conversation had

exhausted him. "Never mind. It's enough. Believe I'm a straitlaced snob, if it makes you happy."

She told him gently, "Well, I suppose you're not really a snob…."

"Enough, I said."

"Very well." She went and stood over him and put her hands on his wonderful, hard shoulders.

He muttered, "Your family is wonderful."

"Yes, they are." She bent and kissed the top of his head.

He groused, "And I've never felt so out of place. Breakfast in the sovereign's apartments. Never in a hundred thousand years…"

"You got through it. And quite gracefully, I thought."

"You're just saying that."

"No. I do mean it. I truly do, Marcus."

He took her right hand from his shoulder then, and pressed his lips to her palm and tipped his head back to look up into her eyes. "Marry me."

She almost said yes right then and there. But she caught herself and gently withdrew her hand. "It's only been four days since you moved in here. I do think that we really need a little more time."

At ten on Monday, Hector Anteros showed up in Marcus's cubicle at CCU headquarters.

He shut the door, eased himself down into Marcus's one extra chair and said, "Am I hearing wedding bells?"

Marcus sent his mentor a weary glance. "I think she has to say yes first. The wedding bells come after."

"So you *have* asked her again?"

"And again. And again."

The space was small. Hector turned the chair so he could stretch out his legs. He groaned a little as he straightened them. "It hurts being old. Take my word for it—or don't. You'll find out for yourself one day."

Marcus closed the report he'd been working on. "You're working up to something. I can always tell. Just say it, whatever it is."

"I'm old."

"I'm clear on that. Go on."

"I find that living with guilt weighs on me."

"All right. You're guilty. Of what?"

Hector didn't look all that guilty. He looked a bit smug, really. He arched a bushy brow in Marcus's direction. "Did you really think that no one knew about you and Her Highness Rhiannon eight years ago?"

Marcus's heart lurched in his chest. His mouth dropped open. "You...? No."

Hector nodded. "At that time, as you are well aware, security was less of a focus. We didn't have round-the-clock protection for Her Highness while she was studying at UCLA. But of course, it was the duty of the Sovereign's Guard to see to her safety. We hired a trustworthy American security team to keep an eye on her, and—once you began spending time with her—on you."

*We?* "Who else knew?"

Hector named two officers of the Sovereign's Guard, good men, and discreet. "And the Americans who reported to us." But Marcus wasn't thinking of his fellow soldiers or the Americans. "Her Sovereign Highness and Prince Evan? Did *they* know?"

Hector gazed at him so calmly. "No."

"But it would have been your duty to—"

"Not necessarily. You see, Her Sovereign Highness made a special point, with each of her sons and daughters once they were of a certain age, to give them the freedom to make their own choices. I was instructed to allow Princess Rhiannon to test her wings, to find her own way as much as possible. It was most important to the sovereign and Prince Evan that their sons and daughters never felt spied upon. In my judgment, you posed neither a danger nor a threat, so I didn't approach the sovereign about what was going on." The explanation did make sense, given what Rhia had always said about her parents giving her the freedom to live her own life.

But that didn't absolve Hector from his responsibility to report what he knew to the sovereign. "You should have told Her Highness Adrienne."

Hector only grinned. "But I didn't. I chose to take my sovereign at her word and protect the privacy of Her Highness Rhiannon. And I don't think you're in any position to judge *my* decisions during that time. It was long ago, and it's over and done—and what happened way back when is not what I've come here to clear my conscience about."

"My God. There's more?"

"Consider. I knew about your past with Her Highness Rhiannon. And yet I was the one who suggested to His Highness Alexander that you be assigned to provide her security for the wedding in Montana."

"*You...?* I don't... You can't..." He seemed to be having difficulty forming actual sentences.

"Yes. I did. I provided, you might say, a window of opportunity for you. And for the princess you could never forget."

Marcus strove for calm as the man he respected most in the world sat there and told him that he had intentionally broken a critical rule. "But...it makes no sense that you would do such a thing. Hector, you know better. It wasn't safe. If you knew that she was important to me, that we had history, then you knew I didn't have the necessary objectivity to protect her effectively."

Hector waved a hand. "Perhaps."

"Hector, it was *wrong*. Dangerous. She ran away from the wedding party because she couldn't stand to be near me. Anything might have happened to her. We were in an auto accident. She could have been hurt. She could have *died*."

"But she wasn't hurt and she didn't die."

Marcus fisted his hands on the desktop to keep from leaping up and wrapping them around Hector's throat. "I have a powerful urge to throttle you, old man."

"Keep your shirt on. Hear me out. Yes, I took a risk."

"A foolish, pointless, dangerous risk."

Hector was unperturbed. "A risk that needed taking. For *both* of your sakes." With another pained groan, he pulled himself to his feet. "I'm an old man. And I'm alone. No wife to nag me, no children to give me grandchildren. I don't especially like being alone and I didn't want that for you. Now, because of what I've set in motion, you *won't* be alone. You will have a family. I don't regret the chance I took."

"Regret? You seem downright proud of yourself."

"Just get her to say yes. Be happy. That's all I'm asking of you."

Marcus gaped up at him. "And now you're leaving? Walking out, just like that? I should file a report on what you just told me."

Hector chuckled merrily. "What? To get me booted from the guard? That would be difficult, as I'm already retired."

"You could lose your position as advisor to the commander."

Hector limped to the door. "Do your worst, Marcus my lad. I'm going home where I can put my feet up."

That night, in the spirit of openness and sharing that Rhia had demanded—and also to ease his conscience a little for continuing to keep his deepest secret from her—Marcus told her what Hector had told him. They were in bed by then and had made slow, satisfying love. She'd already turned out the light and they lay beneath the covers, side by side.

He stared up toward the dark ceiling and told her what Hector had said that day.

When he was finished, she laughed in delight. "Oh, I knew it couldn't be only coincidence that you were assigned to me for that trip."

"It's not anything to laugh over, Rhia. It was a dangerous thing for him to do. A bodyguard cannot be allowed to have any personal relationship with someone he's assigned to protect. He must be cool-headed and objective at all times."

She made a distinctly undignified sound then. "I'm sure you're right."

"There is no doubt that I'm right."

"Well, I think it's very sweet that he wants you to be happy, to have a family, not to be alone. If he did something he shouldn't have, it was for a good reason."

"I should report him."

"Don't you dare."

He rolled to his side then and braced his head on his hand. "You are much too cavalier about this."

She gazed up at him, her eyes shining through the dark. "You're not going to report him. You couldn't do that."

He drew her close against him. "You're right. I couldn't." He smoothed her hair off her forehead. "Marry me." He kissed her.

She kissed him back.

But she didn't say yes.

The next day in the early afternoon, Marcus left for Italy to provide security for Prince Damien, who was speaking at a gala fundraising dinner for the victims of a recent flood. It was only a two-day trip.

Still, Rhia missed him. A lot. Wednesday, she got a call from Montana. Belle was happy in her new life and deeply in love with her new husband. Rhia told her older sister everything at last, about her past with Marcus, about what had happened the night of Belle's wedding and about the coming baby, too.

"So now you two are together," Belle said in a musing tone. "Will you marry him?"

"I want to. So very much. But I need to be sure that it's something that can last."

"I understand." Belle made a soft sound low in her throat. "Marcus. I never guessed it was Marcus that you loved all those years ago…."

"It was a secret he insisted I keep."

"He's a good man, Rhia. Considerate. Trustworthy."

"Yes, I know he is."

"Be happy, Rhia."

"Oh, Belle. I promise you, I'm working on that."

On Thursday evening, Rhia came home from the museum complex to find Marcus waiting for her.

Her heart lifted at the sight of him. She ran to him and he opened his arms to grab her close. He kissed her until her head spun.

And then, his mouth still fused with hers, he lifted her high in his strong arms. He carried her straight to the bedroom, where he swiftly took off all her clothes and showed her that he had missed her, too.

It was only afterward, as they lay there holding each other close beneath the sheet, that she sensed something wasn't right.

She lifted up so she could see his face. "Something's going on. You're much too quiet."

He ran the back of his finger down the side of her arm, stirring goose bumps in his wake. "I'm always quiet."

She wasn't buying. "Uh-uh. There's quiet. And then there's…quiet. You've got something on your mind."

He glanced away.

She caught his beard-rough jaw and made him look at her. "What's happened?"

He drew a much-too-careful breath. "You are not going to like this."

She held his gaze. She refused to let go. "Tell me."

"Before I get into it, I just want you to know that I honestly have been trying to find a way to explain this to you. I thought I would have more time to work up to it. But then, this morning, I found out I really can't afford to put it off any longer."

"Put what off? Marcus, you're scaring me. What are you talking about?"

"Just…wait." He put a finger to her lips, so gently. "Let me say this in my own stumbling way."

"Yes. All right. Of course." She gulped. "Go on."

He started in again. "I've been planning to tell you, trying to figure out how, exactly, to manage it…."

She ached to demand that he tell her and tell her now, but somehow she succeeded in keeping her mouth shut.

And about then, he gave up trying to ease into it. He said simply and flatly, "You're right. There's no good way to say this. I got a call from Los Angeles today. This morning, my father died."

## Chapter Eleven

"B-but you don't *have* a father," she heard herself sputtering. "I mean, do you?"

He pulled away from her, pushed back the sheet and swung his legs over the edge of the bed. And then he just sat there. She stared at his powerful naked back. His big shoulders were hunched.

"Marcus?" She asked his name raggedly, barely making a sound. When he didn't answer, she reached out.

But he was already bending to grab his trousers from the floor. He rose and put them on. For a moment she thought he would pull on the rest of his clothes and walk out, leave her there gaping after him, naked in the bed where they'd just made love.

But then he did turn to her. He held out both arms to the side in a hopeless, bewildered sort of gesture. "All those years ago, I couldn't bear to tell you. I've never told anyone, except the investigators I hired to find out if he really might be who he said he was. The man is…*was* not a father to me in any way that matters. But biologically, yes. He's the man who fathered me."

She had to concentrate to draw breath. "I don't… All those years ago, when we were together, you knew of him then? At UCLA?"

He stuck his hands in his pockets, as though he couldn't decide what exactly to do with them. "Yes."

"But you always said—"

"I know what I said. It was… I couldn't talk about it then. I wanted to forget all about it, about *him*. I wanted it to be as if he'd never approached me, as if I'd never seen his face or heard him tell me I was his son."

"*When,* Marcus? When did he approach you?"

"Just before I first met you."

"In Los Angeles?"

He nodded. He still had his hands in his pockets and he seemed to be looking everywhere but at her. "I had only just arrived in California. He approached me the first day I was there. It was in Westwood. I'd gone to the drugstore to pick up razors and shave cream and toothpaste. He just came right up to me there on Westwood Boulevard. He said he was my father and that he'd hired people to keep track of me through the years, that he had learned of my fellowship at UCLA, had known I would be coming to Southern California. He knew where my dorm was. He said he'd followed me from campus just then…."

His words came at her. She heard them, but as though from far away. Her mind kept cycling back to the impossible fact that he actually knew who his father was. "I don't understand. You never told me. How could you never have told me something so enormous as that?"

"Rhia, I didn't believe him then. I *refused* to believe him, even though I couldn't deny, even on that first day,

that I did look like him. I called him a liar. He grabbed
my hand and put a piece of paper in it. He said if I ever
wanted to know the story of my birth, I should give him
a call. I kept that scrap of paper, but I didn't call. Not for
more than two years. Not until after you came to me and
told me you wanted to try again with me. After that, after
losing you a second time…I don't know why that made the
difference, but then, somehow, I *had* to know."

She longed to correct him, to remind him that he hadn't
*lost* her. *He had sent her away.* But the pain in his voice
stopped her. Yes, he should have told her all of this before. She was shocked and hurt that he hadn't. It cut deep
that he hadn't. It was the harshest sort of proof of the basic
problem she had with him. He kept himself apart. He kept
secrets. She needed to be the one he told his secrets to.

But then she reminded herself that he *was* telling her
his secrets. He was telling her right now. And it was agony
for him.

His suffering broke her heart. She reached out her hand
again. "Come here. Here to me. Please…"

He shook his head. He still didn't look at her. "I hate
this. I should have told you, but I didn't know how. And I
didn't want to think about it, about *him.* It makes me want
to put my fist through a wall, whenever I think about him."

She scooted to the edge of the bed, until she could reach
out and catch his hand. When she did, she pulled him toward her. "Come on. Sit down."

He hovered in place for a moment. But then at last he
came to her and dropped to the mattress. Dragging the
sheet to cover herself, she swung her legs over the edge
so she could sit beside him.

She still had hold of his hand. And now, he was holding
on, too. Tightly. He took her hand into his lap, twined their
fingers together and looked down at them, as though the

sight steadied him somehow. "Eight years ago, I thought I knew who I was. I fully accepted that I was alone, that whoever my parents had been, they had deserted me. For me, they didn't exist. What I would make of my life would be completely of my doing, on my own shoulders. I had graduated from university, had received my commission. You know how rare that is, for a commoner, for someone with no family, to receive an officer's commission?"

She nodded. "Yes. I know. Very rare."

"I was proud, of all I'd done, of how far I had come from such difficult beginnings. I was a university graduate with a commission. I was in America, sent there for a special fellowship…and then a complete stranger walked up to me and said he was my father. It blew my world apart. I considered just…leaving."

"Leaving what?"

"Leaving everything. Vanishing. Disappearing into America."

She pressed herself closer against his side, wishing she could somehow make it better for him. Not so annihilating. Not so full of pain. "But you didn't."

He shook his head again. "It's strange. I was so angry. My fury made me bold. Had I not been so angry, I never would have dared to approach you that day in the bookstore when you challenged me for staring at you. I never would have presumed to introduce myself so brashly, nor to go with you when you asked me to coffee. I never would have gone so far as to stare openly at you when I saw you and knew who you were. If I still hadn't been reeling from that encounter outside the drugstore, if I hadn't been burning with rage and ready for anything, I would have turned carefully on my heel at the very sight of you and walked away. Had you, for some reason, happened to smile upon me, I would have saluted, of course, and given you a proper greeting. But never in any way would I have allowed you to see me as more than a soldier at your command and sworn to serve."

"So then," she tried gamely, doing her best to look on the bright side, "in a way, we have this father of yours to thank, for…bringing us together."

He stared straight ahead. "We have nothing to thank him for. Nothing."

She wrapped her other hand around his bare arm. It was hard as ungiving rock, every muscle tensed. "You never had a chance to make your peace with him, then?"

He glanced at her sharply. "I think I have, yes. As much as I can. I never could forgive him for what he did. But I have accepted that he is—was—the man who fathered me."

"Marcus. You seem…"

"What?" He was looking at her now, his face set in a furious scowl. "I seem what?"

She braved his scowl to answer truthfully. "You seem far from peaceful when you speak of him."

He let out a slow breath. "All right. You have a point, I suppose. No, then. I have never managed to reconcile with him. And I don't imagine I ever could have."

Gently, she asked, "Will you tell me his name?"

"Roland Scala."

"Scala? Is that a Greek name?"

"He became an American citizen more than a decade ago. But he was born here, born Montedoran."

"And your mother…?"

"Her name was Isa Rhodes. She died the night I was born."

"Oh, Marcus. I'm so, so sorry.…"

He gave a shrug. And then, bleakly, he asked, "Are you sure that you want to hear this? It's not a happy story."

She met his gaze steadily. "I do want to hear it, Marcus. Very much."

"Fair enough." He drew in a breath—and then let it out hard. "I don't know where to start."

"Anywhere. It doesn't matter where you start. It only matters that you tell me what happened, how it was...."

He gazed at her for several seconds, unspeaking. And then finally, he blurted, "My mother was a roulette dealer at the casino."

"At Casino d'Ambre?" She named the world-famous casino not far from her villa.

"That's right." He turned his eyes away and stared straight ahead. And then he seemed to gather himself. He started rattling off the story swiftly, as though he couldn't get it out and over with fast enough. "She was half French, half Montedoran. Roland met her there, at the casino. They were lovers. He said that by the time she knew she was pregnant, it was over between them. They didn't marry. He said they were always fighting and they both agreed that they would never make it as a couple. She left Montedoro and went across the border into France when she was six months along."

"To her family?"

"She had no family. Neither did he. They were both only children. With older parents. By the time they met, they were both on their own...." He was quiet. She wanted to prompt him to go on. But she didn't. She waited. And finally he continued, "Two months later, she gave birth to me in a small country hospital. As soon as I was born, that same night, she took me and left the hospital. She went back to the cottage where she'd been living and called Roland. She told him he had a son, and that she'd taken me home with her. He thought she sounded strange, confused. Delirious. So he went to her. She had hemorrhaged, he told me. He claimed she was already dead when he got there. He was afraid to call the authorities. And afraid to just leave me there, for fear no one would find me soon enough and I would die, too. So he took me back to Montedoro...." He seemed to run out of steam.

She finished for him, softly. Regretfully. "And he abandoned you on the steps of Our Lady of Sorrows."

He squeezed her hand harder. "That's right. He abandoned me. And then he went to America right after that. He had some money put by, he said. He gave up gambling. Opened a restaurant. Did well for himself. Applied for citizenship—and got it after he'd been in Southern California for fifteen years."

She pressed her lips to the hard curve of his shoulder, longing to give him comfort, knowing that nothing could ease him right then. "He told you all of this when you finally contacted him six years ago?"

"Yes. I returned to Los Angeles then, and met with him."

"And you believed him, believed his story?"

"Not a word of it. But he showed me the certificate of my birth, which he'd found on the kitchen table in the cottage where my mother bled to death after having me. The birth date was right. She had named Roland as the father. And so I...looked into it. I hired someone to investigate for me. The investigator found out that a woman named Isa Rhodes had died in the place and in the way that Roland said. Though the baby was never found, the district coroner had determined that she'd very recently borne a child and then the local police discovered that she'd given birth in the same hospital named on the certificate my father had taken from the cottage."

"Oh, Marcus." She leaned her head on his shoulder, rubbed her hand up and down his arm. "I don't know what to say. I'm so sorry…for all of it. For your mother and you. And even for your father."

He spoke low and intensely. "Don't feel sorry for him."

"But he—"

"Just don't. He left her there, with no one. All alone, even if it was too late for her. And then he took me…and left me, too."

She wanted to remind him that it was best not to judge. But what did she know about how it must be for him? She'd led a graceful, happy, sheltered life for the most part, with two loving parents who doted on her, with the world at her feet and brothers and sisters she adored. That day she'd told him she was having his baby, he'd called her proud and thoughtless. He'd said she took her happy childhood and her family for granted.

She'd been shocked at the time that he would say such cruel things to her.

But now she saw the truth in his words.

Now she knew that *she* was the one who had no right to judge.

She asked, softly, "He died just today, you said?"

Marcus nodded. "Or late last night. A lawyer contacted me through the CCU several hours ago. He said that Roland had sold his restaurant and retired. That he has a woman, a longtime housekeeper, who comes in to clean and cook for him every day. When the housekeeper went to make up his room, he was just lying there in bed, already gone. The doctor she called said it was some kind of aneurysm or a heart attack. They'll know more later. And I…I am his heir. The lawyer said I should come."

"Of course you must go."

"I don't want to go." He sounded slightly numb. But angry, too. A slow, seething, deep-seated kind of anger. "Why should I go? That man is nothing to me."

"Marcus." He looked at her then. His eyes were flat, the color leached from them. She said, "We'll go together, you and me."

He pulled his hand from hers. "I told you, I don't want to go. And there is no way I could ask you to go. That wouldn't be right."

"Of course it's right. And you're not asking me. *I'm* asking *you*. Please. Take me with you. Let's do this together. Let me be with you for this."

He put his head in his hands. "I don't want to do this."

"Marcus, you have to. You know that you do."

"No. I don't know that. I don't know that at all." He raised his head and looked at her wildly. "I don't want any of this. I haven't spoken with that man in over five years. I thought I had…accepted the reality that he was my biological father. But I certainly didn't want him in my life. I *am* the man I was raised to be. I am Marcus Desmarais. I own that name and I earned it. I never planned to tell a soul about him. Until you. Until now, in this past week…" He fell silent. His eyes were haunted now, guarded. And furious, too. But he did lift a hand. He cradled the side of her face. She melted inside at the tender touch. "Because you demanded that I tell you my secrets…."

She held his gaze. "I'm so glad that you've told me. I only wish you had told me sooner."

"I didn't want to tell you at all." The words were rough, very low.

She gazed steadily at him and didn't even try to hide her reproach. "Always guarding your secrets, so self-contained…"

He surprised her by answering with urgency. "But I swear to you, Rhia. I knew I needed to tell you. I *was* working up to it."

In spite of her frustration with him, she found she believed him—and she said so. "I believe you. And it does help me, Marcus, when you tell me the hardest things, the things you wish you could keep secret even from yourself."

He made a scoffing sound and dropped his caressing hand. "Helps you? How could knowing all this…this ugliness possibly help you?"

"It helps me to *know* you, to understand you better."

He grunted. "Why would you ever want to understand a nasty mess like this one?"

"Because that's what you do, when you care for someone. That's what you do for the ones of your family. You listen when they are able to tell you the truth about themselves, no matter how hard that truth might be. And then you do what you can to help them get through whatever difficult time might follow."

## Chapter Twelve

The next morning, early, Marcus went with Rhia to the Prince's Palace to speak with HSH Adrienne.

He told the whole awful story all over again—to his sovereign this time. As always, the princess was serene and understanding and ready to smooth the way. He was given open-ended family leave from his duties at the CCU.

Back at the villa, Rhia called her director at the National Museum and explained that she would be out of the country for a while on urgent family business. Marcus called Roland's lawyer again and said they were coming. And then they packed their suitcases and flew to Los Angeles.

They arrived at LAX after midnight. A car was waiting to take them to the Beverly Wilshire, where a suite had been reserved for them. After they had checked in, Marcus stood on the balcony and stared out over the lights of Beverly Hills and Century City and wondered why he had come. He thought of Lieutenant Joseph Chastain, who had a small room adjacent to their suite and had been assigned to provide security during this trip. Marcus almost envied Joseph.

Joseph was a good man. And he knew exactly what he was here for. He would protect Her Serene Highness with his life. So very simple. So very clear.

Marcus would do the same for Rhia. But as her lover, the father of her child and possibly her future husband—if she ever said yes to him—he would never again be assigned to protect her. A bodyguard needed a cool head, after all, and that all-important emotional distance from the one he was charged with protecting.

Marcus had no emotional distance when it came to Rhiannon. He never had. But in the past, no one else had known—well, except for Hector and Her Highness Alice.

Now, everyone knew. Even the tabloids.

He heard light footsteps as she came out onto the balcony and stood at his side.

"Such a beautiful night." She took his arm and together they admired the view. He enjoyed the feel of her body so close, the touch of her fingers against his skin. He was treated to a faint, tempting hint of her perfume. But soon enough, she was pulling him back inside. "Let's go to bed. We have to be up early tomorrow." The lawyer had agreed to meet with them first thing in the morning, even though it was Saturday.

He stopped just inside the balcony doors and turned her to face him. "It's past 2:00 a.m., already tomorrow."

She gazed up at him, dark hair shining in the lamplight, brown eyes infinitely soft. "We can get a few hours of sleep, at least."

He knew she was right. She needed her rest. But he needed…her. He gathered her close and kissed her.

She opened for him, sighing. And then she tried to pull away.

He didn't allow that, but instead deepened the kiss, holding her even closer, wrapping his arms so tightly around her, using the taste and the feel of her, the wonderful scent that belonged only to her, to help him forget all the things he would have to remember when daylight came.

Eventually, he did lift his head. She stared up at him dreamily and whispered in a tender tone, "Marcus. Bedtime..." Taking his hand, she turned for the bedroom.

He didn't argue with her. She was leading him exactly where he wanted to go. Once they reached the side of the bed, he took off all her clothes and his own, as well, kissing her as he did it, caressing her tenderly, with practiced care.

By the time he was finished undressing them both, she wasn't thinking about sleeping, either. He took her down to the pillows and he kissed her some more. He touched her, the way he liked best to touch her.

Slowly. Everywhere.

Until she was pliant and eager, flushed and so willing— willing in every way except one.

She still wouldn't marry him.

But he would not despair. No matter how many times she told him no, he would never give up. His child would have a father who never, ever gave him up.

And she? No, he couldn't give her all the things she so richly deserved. But he would always protect her, always take care of her. He would be there, at her side, anytime she needed him. He would never arrive too late, never *not* be there when she needed him the most....

Turning her so she lay on her side, facing him, he traced a hand over the marvelous curve of her hip, sliding his palm along the taut smoothness of her thigh, lifting her knee and wrapping her leg over his.

She was so wet, so soft and sweet and ready, and she moaned when he pushed into her, moaned and canted her body up to him, taking him in all the way with that first stroke—at which point he couldn't hold back a moan of his own.

The sweetness, as always with her, was close to unbearable, the way any extreme pleasure tends to be. He had to go carefully, slowly, deliberately, had to try and be mindful of making it last, while his body constantly threatened to throw off all restraint and make that mad dash for the quick, hard finish.

He didn't want that.

He wanted more of her sighs and her soft, tender cries.

And he had them. They rocked together, arms wrapped around each other, for a fine, endless time.

He watched the finish come over her, saw the deep flush that flowed up her throat and over her cheeks, the glazed sheen in her almost-black eyes. Her breathing quickened, became a little bit frantic, and her hips jerked against him, harder, faster, with a sudden furious, hungry intent.

By then, he was gone, too, lost in the fine, swift rhythm she set. She cried out and pressed strongly against him. He held on tight as the rush of his climax shuddered through him.

It was perfect. Satisfying. Exactly what he needed.

But then, it always had been with her.

She took him to paradise so easily, brought him the best kind of forgetfulness. At least for a little while.

The lawyer's name was Anthony Evans. They met him in front of a Century City highrise. He was tall, tanned and fit, with silver hair. He grabbed Marcus's hand and pressed a business card into it. Then he turned a gleaming white smile on Rhia. "Hello."

She murmured her first name and took the hand he offered. He glanced past her shoulder at Joseph. She gave a
light laugh. "That's Joseph. He provides security." At the
mention of his name, the bodyguard gave a slight nod.
Rhia added, "I promise you, Anthony, Joseph won't be
in the way."

Anthony's office was on the top floor of the high-rise.
They sat in fat leather chairs in a large conference room—
except for Joseph, who stood near the door. Anthony explained that he and Roland often played golf together, that
he'd met Roland more than two decades ago at City Bistro,
the restaurant Marcus's father had owned.

"Your father had a very special kind of genius," Anthony said. "He made every customer feel special. Valued.
And he had a hell of a memory. The second time I ate at
the Bistro, he knew the table I preferred and that I wanted
Glenfiddich neat the minute my butt hit the chair."

Marcus had no idea what to say in response to that, so
he didn't say anything.

Rhia, sitting beside him, slipped her hand into his,
twined their fingers companionably together and made
the right noises. "This is all such a shock to everyone."

"Ahem, yes, well," said Anthony. "Difficult. Very difficult. My condolences. Roland will be missed." He put on a
pair of reading glasses and gestured at the folder with the
ring of keys on top of it that waited on the table in front
of Marcus. "Your copy of your father's will. It's all quite
self-evident. Except for a small bequest to the housekeeper,
everything goes to you. The house, the cars, the cabin in
the Sierras—and the money, of course. Your father was a
canny investor."

*The house, the cars, the money.* Marcus heard the words
and realized he could very well be a wealthy man now.

He really wished it mattered more.

Anthony was still talking. "It's all in there." He gestured at the folder again. "Roland asked that there be no funeral service and that he be cremated, that the ashes be entrusted to you and that you scatter them off the coast of Montedoro, in the Mediterranean Sea."

Ashes. He was expected to scatter Roland's ashes?

Rhia squeezed his hand. He saw that Anthony was looking expectantly at him.

So he nodded again. "All right. Yes. Of course."

"The autopsy will be performed by the first of the week, though it's merely a formality, due to the unexpected nature of the death. Once that's done, the remains will be transported to the Neptune Society. You can give them a call and they will tell you when you can come for the ashes."

"All right."

"And you've been to the house, I'm sure…"

He started to nod automatically, but then the words actually registered. "No. I haven't."

If that surprised Anthony, he didn't show it. "Ah. Well, it's no problem. There's a list in the inside pocket of the folder. Addresses, phone numbers, bank accounts, alarm codes. Everything you need to know. Your father seems to have assumed you will be selling the various properties." *Your father.* Marcus longed to tell the lawyer not to call Roland that. But what would that prove, ultimately? Nothing. Anthony asked, "Is that the plan?"

"Yes, I think so."

"Excellent. Because it's all set up that way. Roland's real estate broker will be contacted Monday to arrange to put the house and the Sierra cabin on the market. But still, it's all up to you now. Your father made it very clear that if you want the house, or anything else, you only have to say so and we'll make the necessary arrangements and adjustments."

"Thank you."

"And you have the keys."

Marcus glanced blankly at the folder again, and the keys that waited on top of it. "Yes. I see."

"Anything else, any questions, you have my number. Do not hesitate to call."

A few minutes later, they stood on the sidewalk on sun-lit Century Boulevard. Rhia's driver pulled the limousine up to the curb at the sight of them. Joseph opened the door.

"Back to the hotel?" she asked him once they were safely inside behind the tinted windows.

"Yes, all right."

She took his hand again, scooted over next to him and put her head on his shoulder. He took comfort from the feel of her so close and thought about what a fine, good woman she was. Thought about all she deserved and all she meant to him.

And how he devoutly wished he might be…more, in so many ways.

At least he would have his own money now. If she ever said yes, he wouldn't have to live the rest of his life with her paying for everything. Too bad it was money that came from the man who'd abandoned both him and his mother. There was certainly some very rich irony in that.

His pride and his anger kept jabbing him to refuse it all. To call Anthony Evans and tell him he'd changed his mind, he wanted every penny of Roland's fortune turned over to St. Stephen's Orphanage in Montedoro.

But then he thought of the child. In the end, Roland's money would benefit the child, as well as allow him, Marcus, to contribute in a meaningful way to the financial support of his family.

That meant he couldn't indulge his anger and simply give it all away.

Once in the suite again, he sat down at the desk in the sitting room and read the will through. It was all true, what Anthony had said. There *was* a lot of money. There were a lot of *things*.

It would be enough that he could make a generous bequest to St. Stephen's *and* have plenty left for the baby's future, for Rhia.

And as Anthony had promised, Roland had it all worked out. Marcus didn't really have to do anything. If he took no action, everything would be sold and the money, in time, would be his, the funds transferred to the Bank of Montedoro into an account that had already been set up in his name.

Roland's only request was that Marcus would dispose of the damn ashes off the coast of Montedoro.

In the other room, he heard Rhia talking on the phone. He closed the folder and pushed back his chair, rising to his feet as she appeared from the bedroom.

She came to him, put her hands on his shoulders. "Well?"

He shrugged. "I am quite well-to-do now, as it turns out."

She smiled, but her eyes were sad for him. "I wish that I might have met him." He didn't know what to say to that, so he said nothing. And she soothed, gently, "Never mind." With a shake of her dark head, she brushed a kiss against his lips. "Do you want to visit your father's house?"

"I don't know. Maybe tomorrow. Or the next day." *Or maybe never.* "Who was that on the phone?"

"I talked to Allie. She sends her best. And then to my

mother. She wishes you well and wants you to know she keeps you close in her thoughts. And did I tell you I have Bravo relatives here in Los Angeles?"

"I remember. Jonas and Emma Bravo."

"They were wonderful to me when I was at UCLA. They invited me over for dinner often. I asked you to come with me once, if you'll recall. But you refused. Because we were a secret."

Her hair was down, the way he liked it best. He eased his fingers under the silky mass and clasped the nape of her neck, loving the feel of her skin, and the way the warm strands brushed the back of his hand.

He reminded her, "Keeping what we shared a secret was the only way for me then."

She pressed her lips together and hitched up her chin in that proud way of hers. "I hated it, that secret. The lies. Pretending for all those years that I hardly knew you. Everyone in the family knew that there was…someone. Someone I couldn't get over. Someone who had broken my heart."

He pulled her close, pressed his lips to her forehead. "I'm sorry, Rhia. You can't know how very sorry." He breathed the apology against her skin—and knew that it wasn't enough, that it couldn't make up for all he had put her through.

She tipped her head back to look at him again. Her eyes flashed dark fire. "I'm still angry about that, about the way you demanded that no one could ever know."

"It was a long time ago. Can't we let it go?"

Apparently not. She pinched up her mouth at him. "You mean the way *you* let things go? By refusing to speak of them. By…denying their existence? By walking away and not looking back?" She brought her hands up between them and pushed at his chest.

He released her. "My faults and sins are endless, I know it."

"Please don't become noble on me. I can't bear it right now."

How had they gotten here? A few minutes ago, she'd been all smiles, asking him so thoughtfully if he might want to visit Roland's house. He frowned down at her. "Is this a big fight we're working up to here?"

She remained defiant. "Maybe a big fight would clear the air."

He shut his eyes for a moment, drew in a slow breath. "Please, Rhia. I don't want to fight with you. I only want a chance to care for you, to help raise the child we made. I only want to be your husband."

Her mouth trembled then. She looked away. When she met his eyes again, he saw that her fury and defiance had fled. "You're doing the best you can, I know that. And it's been an awful day for you. I suppose the last thing you need is a hard time from me. That would be...unfair, I do realize. After all, I told you I was coming here to help."

He touched her hair again. She didn't pull away. He said gruffly, "I'm glad you're here."

Her brows drew together. "It's strange. More difficult than I imagined. Being here in Los Angeles again, where we met. Where we...loved so long ago."

"Too difficult?" Was she saying she didn't want to stay?

"I didn't say that."

"But you—"

She stopped him with a finger to his lips. "It may not have seemed like it a moment ago, but I do want to be here. I want it very much."

He wondered if he would ever understand the way a woman's mind worked. "You're certain?"

"Yes. And I spoke with Emma Bravo after I talked to

Mother and Allie. Emma has invited us to her house for dinner tonight."

Just what he needed. To spend the evening making idle chitchat with her Los Angeles relatives. "I don't feel like going out."

"We're going. Live with it."

He was grateful that she'd put aside her anger over the past. And that she really did seem to want to be here with him, to see him through the grim task of dealing with Roland's sudden death. Plus, he knew she was right about the dinner with her Bravo relatives. Sometimes a man just had to get out and deal with other people, no matter how disconnected from his real life he might feel. "Fair enough. Dinner with the Bravos. I cannot wait."

"That's what I needed to hear." She said it cheerfully and he realized he felt better about everything. "But we have hours until then. I think we should try and forget all our problems, all the sadness over Roland, the stress and the worries. What do you say? The pool? The beach?"

He traced the V-neck of the light blouse she wore, and remembered that she used to have a blouse something like it eight years ago. He had a quick, vivid image of her pulling that other blouse over her head, and her long hair crackling with static, lifting and then falling to curl on her shoulders as she tossed the blouse onto the rickety chair in the corner of the bedroom in the motel where they used to go. "Do you ever think of La Casa de la Luna?"

She scanned his face, her eyes seeming brighter suddenly, a glowing smile lighting her up from within. "I do. I have. Often—and let's do that, then. Let's go see how much has changed at the House of the Moon."

"I wasn't really thinking we should go there."

"But why not?"

"You said yourself that it's hard enough being here in Los Angeles, where it all started for us."

"No. Seriously, Marcus. I think we should go. I want to see if it's still the same...."

He realized that she was determined. And he *had* brought it up. Maybe it wouldn't be so bad. "A lot can happen in eight years. We should check first to make sure it hasn't been torn down."

She whipped out her smart phone and punched up the name. And then she grinned and turned the phone so he could see the display. "Still there. Let's go."

"It looks smaller, don't you think?" she asked when they stood on the sidewalk at the front of the Spanish-style motor hotel, with the limo waiting behind them and Joseph standing there at attention by the backseat door.

"Looks about the same to me." Aside from the fact that the stucco walls had more cracks than he remembered and the landscaping seemed a bit more overgrown.

She leaned her shoulder against his. "Let's try and get our room."

He wrapped an arm around her and whispered into her hair, "It won't be the same."

"Oh, Marcus. I know. I don't care. It's not supposed to be the same. Please."

So he signaled to Joseph, who led the way up the chipped tile steps. The bodyguard entered the lobby first to have a quick look around. A moment later, he opened the door for them and they joined him inside, where a rangy white cat lay in a pool of sunshine on the red tile floor and a different clerk stood behind the front desk, an old man with a white scruff of beard and a sour expression on his lined face.

"How can I help you?" The old fellow craned to the side

and peered around them at Joseph, who stood patiently over near the door, in front of a display rack full of brochures of things to do in Los Angeles.

"Is room one-twelve available?" Rhia asked.

The old man frowned. "Might be. But I'm not putting more than two in that room."

Rhia slid Marcus a glance. They both tried not to laugh. And she said, "Oh, that's not a problem." She tipped her head in the bodyguard's direction. "Joseph provides security. He will have to go in the room and give it a quick once-over, but then he will wait outside for us until we're ready to leave."

"Security?" The ancient fellow made a scoffing sound. "Come on, lady. You think you really need security?"

"Apparently, I do." She smiled at him sweetly. "May we have the room?" With a flourish, she indicated Marcus and then herself. "Just the two of us, I promise you."

The old man grumbled, but he let them have the room. Marcus paid for it with cash. They went out and along the central walkway to the room, where Joseph entered first.

They waited down the steps from the door. The birds of paradise were still there, to either side of the steps. They'd grown quite large and the birdlike flowers on their long stems sprouted wildly, hanging over the concrete walk, begging for a good pruning. Back at the entrance, the old man stuck his head out the lobby door, probably to make sure that no threesomes were being committed on his watch.

Finally Joseph emerged. "Safe and clear."

He came out and they went in.

Rhia headed straight for the cheap, scratched-up desk in the corner. "Same desk, remember?"

He did remember. In his mind's eye, he could still see her, sitting in the hard-seated chair, wearing cutoff jeans and a snug little shirt, one foot tucked under her, an art history book open on the table in front of her.

She wandered into the bedroom alcove, where the deep purple-red bougainvillea blazed on the far wall outside the window, just as it had eight years before. The worn-out box springs made squeaky sounds as she sat on the end of the bed. "I was imagining we might make wild, crazy love here, for old times' sake...."

He went and sat beside her. She'd pinned up her hair before they left the hotel, but a dark curl had already escaped and trailed along the side of her neck. He coiled it around his index finger. "Wild and crazy love sounds good to me. But why do I get the feeling you're not really in the mood?"

She sighed then. "It all looks a little...forlorn, somehow."

"It's just more proof that we can never go back."

Her slim shoulders slumped. "Ugh. More sadness. This was not my plan."

The curl of hair kept a corkscrew shape when he pulled his finger free. He wrapped an arm around her. "It's all right." She looked up at him and he kissed the tip of her aristocratic nose. "I *have* always wondered what became of the place."

She was studying him again. "Yes, well. There is that."

"Now we know." He wanted to kiss her, to say, *Marry me.* He'd bought a ring on Tuesday, before leaving for Italy with Prince Damien, and he was carrying it with him everywhere, waiting for the right moment.

Unfortunately, he had to admit that now probably wasn't it.

And then she asked, "Did you ever plan to marry and have a family, Marcus—I mean, marry someone else, before Montana and the baby?"

He didn't want to tell her. So he hedged. "Does it matter?"

She stood up and went to the window. For a moment, she stared out at the bougainvillea across the way. When she turned to face him, her eyes were stormy again, the way they'd been back at the hotel. "It matters. Yes."

Why? She didn't need to hear about the life he wasn't going to have now. "I don't agree. What matters is you and me. The baby…"

She made a circuit of the room, ending back at the window again. For a moment, she stared out. Then she faced him. "I keep waiting for you to see, to understand that I need to know…all about you. You keep telling me how you're going to be more open with me. And then, well, every time I ask you something about your life, about the past, about your dreams for yourself, you brush me off like I'm lint on your sleeve."

That was unfair. He stood. "That's not so."

"Yes. Yes, it *is* so." She wrapped her arms around herself in a protective sort of way. "I want…more than just a husband, Marcus. I want *you.* I want you in the deepest, truest way. I wish you could see that."

"I don't want to hurt you."

She blew out an impatient breath. "I can take a little hurting now and then. A little pain is worth it. Sometimes it's more important to know the truth than to be protected from the things that I might not especially enjoy hearing."

"But it doesn't even matter."

"How many times do I have to say it? Yes. It does matter. It matters to *me.*"

By then, Marcus ardently wished he had just answered her question in the first place. He'd made way too much of it and now she was watching him with real anxiety, expecting some horrible revelation that would change everything.

So he went ahead and admitted, "I did plan to marry, yes. Eventually."

She gasped. "Oh, no." Her voice was much too soft, her eyes wide now, and worried. "I can't believe I was so selfish. I can't believe that I never even bothered to ask."

"Ask what?" He felt like a blind man plunked down in an unknown room, groping madly to gain some familiarity with the alien space.

"That night, I... Oh, Marcus, it was just all about *me,* you know? All about what *I* needed to get through what was happening. It never even occurred to me that you might have... Oh, God. I just feel terrible about this."

He dared to reveal his complete ignorance. "Do you know that I haven't a clue what you're talking about?"

She came and dropped down beside him again. "That night in Montana..."

"Er, what about it?"

"Marcus, was there someone you were seeing then, someone you had to end it with because of what happened with us?"

## Chapter Thirteen

It was something of a relief to hear the question at last, because the answer was easy. "No, of course not. I wasn't seeing anyone."

She put a hand to her chest and blew out a breath. "Oh, thank God."

"Why would you imagine such a thing? Yes, it's true that I haven't been as forthcoming as I should have been…"

She actually rolled her eyes. "Understatement of the decade. I mean, given that we're here in America right now to settle the estate of the father you never mentioned that you had."

"But you must see. Roland is one thing."

"Roland is a very *big* thing."

"Rhia. If there was another woman, you can be sure I would have told you. I would have told you that night, under the blankets in the backseat of that SUV before things went too far. I would have told you and that would have stopped it. Not only because I would not betray someone who trusted me, but also because you would never have made love with me if you thought I had someone else."

"You make me sound like a model of integrity when I just admitted that I wasn't thinking about anyone but myself."

He hooked an arm across her shoulders. "You couldn't do that to another woman. It's just not in you."

Reaching up, she brushed soft fingers against his cheek. "But you did plan to get married?"

Better, he saw now, just to tell her straight out. "Yes. I thought I would find a kind, even-tempered woman of my own class, someone who would look up to me, a woman who would be thoroughly impressed with my success and proud of my accomplishments, someone who wanted to raise a family."

Her mouth trembled a little. She asked, "So you thought you would marry some stranger just because she would look up to you?"

"Well, my hope was that she wouldn't be a stranger by the time that I asked her to be my wife."

She chuckled then. "Oh, Marcus." He pulled her closer and she settled companionably into the crook of his arm. "I always hoped you would be happy, I truly did. I just never wanted to imagine the particulars."

"Yet you asked…"

"Because I really did want to know."

Actually, he understood her conflicting emotions on this subject. It had been the same for him. "Both of those times you were engaged?"

She put a hand over her eyes. "Do you *have* to remind me?"

"I told myself how I *should* be happy for you—and then I went and took on all comers in the training yard."

She blinked. "Fighting, you mean?"

"A soldier has to keep in shape. And proficiency at hand-to-hand combat is part of the necessary skill set. Plus, well, hand-to-hand in the ring is the one place where rank doesn't matter. We're all equal there. As we are a small force, we have to practice on each other. Challenges are open to everyone in the guard and the CCU, so I had a good number of opponents to spar with and no end of opportunities to pound some heads."

"You're telling me that when I became engaged, you beat up your comrades in arms."

"All in the interest of peak fitness and battle-readiness, of course."

"Oh, yes. Of course." She slanted him a knowing look. "Did you take on those two we met on the Promenade last week, Denis and Rene?"

He hesitated to answer. He'd never carried tales. He'd taken his knocks and kept his mouth shut. But now, after finally telling her about Roland, after making himself admit that he had always planned to marry someone else, he was beginning to see why she asked for his secrets.

It was a way to bind them, each to the other. She should be the one in the world he could trust with the things he would never tell anyone else.

So he confessed, "As a matter of fact, Denis and Rene were first in line."

"Did you win your bouts with them?"

"I did, yes. I wish I could say I found those victories satisfying. But thrashing an old nemesis or two didn't change anything that mattered. You were still about to become another man's wife."

She made a small, throaty sound. "And then I didn't marry either of my fiancés, after all. I couldn't bring myself to do it. Both times I ended up having to admit that it wasn't going to work."

"And I was glad," he said low and rough.

She turned those shining eyes to him then. "I'll bet you hated yourself for that."

"I did. It was wrong. I had given you up twice. I had no right to be glad when you didn't find the happiness I kept telling myself I wanted for you. And I did want it. I *wanted* you to be happy—I just didn't want to think of you with anyone else."

Tenderly, she said, "We are ludicrous." They were the exact words she'd used the day she told him about the baby. Only now, somehow, the meaning was altogether different. Fond. And also gentle. Like the touch of Sister Lucilla's hand at St. Stephen's, when he was small. The sister would clasp his shoulder and smile benignly down at him and he would feel…blessed somehow. Reassured that in the end, though his birth parents had abandoned him and his adoptive parents had sent him back, though he had nobody to call his own, everything would come out right in the end.

Rhia suggested softly, "You know I want to know more about those two men you grew up with, about St. Stephen's, about your childhood there…."

He reconciled himself to giving her what she needed from him: another large dose of sharing. "It wasn't a bad childhood, really. In spite of what you hear about nuns at Catholic orphanages, the nuns who raised me were mostly kind. Then again, I was one of the good boys. I had no one and the only way I could see to make anyone care for me or pay attention to me was to be very, very good. The nuns approved of me."

"And Denis and Rene?"

"They got attention by making trouble and they were always suffering the consequences, forever being punished for some transgression or other. And they hated me. They were constantly engineering opportunities to make me pay for being a kiss-up."

"What ways?"

"Just the usual things that bad boys do to good ones."

"Such as?"

"Once they nearly drowned me in a toilet. They also lured me into the catacomb of cellars beneath St. Stephen's and then locked me down there in the dark. They stole my schoolbooks and my finished assignments and then destroyed them. And they beat me up every chance they got."

She made a low, outraged sound, as women tend to do when hearing stories of boys' inhumanity to boys. "That's terrible. You didn't fight back?"

"At first, yes. But I quickly learned that fighting back was an exercise in futility. They only beat me harder. So I would run away as fast as I could whenever I saw them coming. If I wasn't fast enough to escape, I would curl into a ball and bear whatever punishments they meted out. It went on like that for several years until I was strong enough to win my fights with them."

"Did you tell the nuns what they were doing to you?"

He gave her a patient look. "No."

"Well, you should have."

"Rhia, I survived. And I grew stronger. I started working out, studying up on martial arts and boxing. I was fifteen when I first took them both on and won. After that, they mostly left me alone."

"But they resent you to this day."

"How would I know? It's nothing I would ever discuss with them. And I have no way of knowing what goes on in their heads."

"Oh, of course you do. We all have instincts about such things."

"Yes, but now that I'm a grown man and not the least afraid of either of them anymore, I'm not especially interested in knowing what Denis and Rene are thinking."

She gave that some thought. And then she slid out from under his arm and stood.

He caught her hand before she could completely escape him. "Stay here."

She stepped up nice and close and he spread his thighs a little so she could ease in between them. Bracing her hands on his shoulders, tipping her head to the side, she studied him the way she often did. "I think that you are tired of sharing."

"You could say that, yes."

She leaned down to him. He breathed in the scent of her and thought about how fine she looked naked, how swiftly he'd become accustomed to being naked with her on a regular basis.

How he really would like to be naked with her right now.

But the room had a faint smell of mildew and the bed-springs creaked. He couldn't help wondering how clean the bedding was. They had some fine memories in Room 112. Making a new one right now?

He didn't think so.

She kissed the space between his eyebrows. "I'm ready to go if you are."

They continued their trip down memory lane. Visiting the places where they had been together before seemed to please her and he wanted very much to please her.

It also helped to keep his mind off the father who had deserted his mother and him.

The father he would never see again.

Not that he *wanted* to see Roland again. He didn't. Of course not.

They went to the bookstore at UCLA, the one where they'd met. And then for lunch, they tried the hamburger stand where they used to eat all the time way back when. They had cheeseburgers and fries and vanilla milkshakes and agreed that the greasy, heavy food was every bit as good as it had been eight years ago.

"When it comes to cheeseburgers," Rhia said, "you *can* relive the past."

They returned to the hotel for their swimsuits and went to Seal Beach, where they spent the afternoon slathered in sunscreen, basking on beach towels and wading in the surf, with the silent Joseph keeping watch.

That evening, they visited the Bravos at their estate, Angel's Crest, in Bel Air. Emma and Jonas had four children—two boys and two girls. They were also raising Jonas's adopted sister, Amanda, who was sixteen, something of a musical prodigy and stunningly beautiful, with enormous dark eyes and curly black hair.

Emma was a blonde charmer from a small town in Texas and Jonas doted on her. Their sons were three and seven and their daughters ten and five and Emma clearly believed that children should be both seen *and* heard. The children came to the table for dinner and laughter and happy chatter filled the elegant formal dining room.

The three-year-old, Grady, was an especially enthusiastic talker. He sat right up at the table in a booster chair. Marcus ended up seated on his right. Grady told him all about his plastic dinosaur collection and explained in great and nearly incomprehensible detail what levels he had reached playing Angry Birds.

Later that night, when they were alone together in the

hotel suite, Marcus told Rhia, "I liked them—Jonas and his wife, the children, Amanda, *all* of them."

They'd kicked off their shoes and stood barefoot on the balcony, admiring the lights of the city that spread out like a blanket of stars all the way to the Santa Monica Mountains. "I think you had a good time tonight," she said. "Though you didn't expect to."

"I assumed it would be four adults at a candlelit table making polite conversation. I had no idea there would be all those children, everyone talking over everyone else. It was all so energetic. And there was so much laughter, wasn't there?"

"Yes, there was."

"Was it like that when you were small?" Somehow, he'd never pictured the princely family being rambunctious at dinner.

"Often it was, yes. We would argue sometimes, and we would all grow excited. Except for Max. Maybe it was because he was the oldest. He always stayed in control and would try to calm us down. Damien was the biggest troublemaker. Once he grabbed the bread basket and began firing dinner rolls at Alexander, who then jumped up, ran around the table and punched Damien in the nose."

"Was there blood?"

"A river of it. Genevra, always so tenderhearted, became very upset and started crying." Genevra was eighth-born of the nine Bravo-Calabretti siblings.

Marcus laughed. "You will destroy all my illusions of the way young royals behave."

"I told you all this, didn't I, years ago?"

He took her by the shoulders, pulled her in front of him and wrapped his arms around her waist. "No."

She leaned back into him, resting her hands on his forearms. "We didn't talk enough, then—although, when I

think back, I remember that I did feel close to you, closer
than I ever have to anyone else, really."

"We were so young."

"And you were so incommunicative."

"Rhia, it was only eight weeks. And we spent a lot of
the time we had together in that creaky bed at La Casa
de la Luna."

"We always did communicate well with our clothes
off, didn't we?"

He pressed his lips to her hair. "Yes, we did."

She stared dreamily out toward the mountains. "It was
all just so heart-stoppingly romantic, that time. And I did
talk about my family then, didn't I?"

"A bit. I seem to recall your telling me about the plays
that you and your sisters and Princess Liliana used to put
on."

"Yes. The plays were glorious—or at least, we thought
so. Belle wrote most of them. They were full of princesses
and knights and fire-breathing dragons. We made our own
costumes. Our brothers and our parents and any available
servants were called upon to be the audience. It was great
fun. Oh, and we all enjoyed board games, too. We were
quite competitive, especially the boys and Allie. In a horse
race or a game of Risk, you will never beat Allie."

He bent to kiss the side of her neck and flattened a palm
against her belly. Was it a fraction rounder than before?

She put her hand over his. "I watched you with Grady.
You were wonderful."

"I was trying to keep up with what he was telling me
and not exactly succeeding."

"I think you did very well."

He remembered that he was supposed to tell her the
things that were hard to admit. "In the past couple of

weeks, since you told me about the baby, I find I think about being a father. I think about it a lot."

She turned in his arms and gazed up at him steadily. "You're worried about this, about being a good father?"

He shrugged. "Maybe a little."

"Because you were raised without one?"

He nodded. "And don't start feeling sorry for me."

"I don't." A smile flirted with the corners of her mouth. "But I do feel some sympathy for the lonely and oh-so-well-behaved little boy you once were...."

"Rein it in."

"You will be a fine father. Because you *want* to be a good father. And that means you will work very hard to be one."

"I hope you're right."

"I know I am." She spoke with absolute assurance.

And then she lifted up on tiptoe and kissed him.

When she sank back to her heels once more, he said roughly, "Do that again."

She did. By then, he was hungry for the kind of communicating they'd always done so effortlessly. He picked her up by the waist. She wrapped those fine legs around him and he turned and carried her back inside.


The next day was Sunday. They called room service for breakfast.

As she poured him a second cup of coffee, he said, "I think I want to go to Roland's house today."

She didn't seem surprised. "Yes. Let's do that."

So her driver took them to Beverly Hills. The house was behind a tall stone fence covered in ivy, with an electronic gate. Marcus read the gate code to the driver and he leaned out the window and punched up the numbers on the keypad built into the wall. The gate slid open and they rode up a curving cobbled driveway with thick lawns and beautifully tended semitropical landscaping to either side.

"So green," Rhia said. "Beautiful and private."

The house was a one-story midcentury modern. The front door locked with another keypad. Marcus entered the numbers from the list of codes Anthony had provided. Joseph went in and Marcus read off the alarm code for him.

Once Joseph had vouched for their safety within, they entered. The slate-floored foyer opened onto a living room with a wall of windows looking out on the backyard. It was all very clean and attractive and well-maintained.

Rhia took his arm. He led her forward, into the bright central room, to the dining area and the modern kitchen, with its granite counters and stainless-steel appliances. She opened the refrigerator.

Empty. Spotless. She tried the door between two gleaming countertops. It was a pantry. There were rows of canned goods, dried pasta and boxed cereal.

"I do believe these cans are alphabetized," she said, and shut the door.

He went to another door. It opened to a laundry room. A door beyond that went to the three-car garage. He flipped on the light out there. A Jaguar, a Mercedes and a Land Rover, each one shiny and new. He could hardly bear to look at them. He turned off the light and quickly shut the door.

She was waiting in the kitchen. "Marcus, are you all right?" She searched his face.

He muttered, "Let's just go through the rest of it."

"All right." She followed him out of the kitchen and down a long hallway with a study, three bedrooms and two baths branching off it. The rooms were painted in deep colors—reds and forest greens, jewel blues and deep browns. Overall, the impression was inviting, Marcus thought, and attractive. He hated it, every inch of it.

"It's all so impersonal," Rhia said sadly. "Not a single snapshot of a friend or any family photographs. And all the art has that look."

"What look?"

"Generic. As though he bought it all framed and properly matted at some gift shop or art emporium."

They entered the big bedroom at the end of the hall. The room was a deep maroon color, with plain, dark, well-made furniture. Marcus knew from the size of it and the full bath branching off it that it must be the master suite. There was a sitting area and a sliding door led out to a small patio. He set the list of codes and the ring of keys on the sitting area table and opened the walk-in closet, which had been designed for maximum use of the space. Roland's clothing hung so neatly. All the shoes were clean and polished, lined up with soldierly precision.

"Everything is so neat and tidy," Rhia said from behind him. "The housekeeper even made the bed. It's hard to believe a man died here just three days ago."

He stared at the long row of dress shirts, each perfectly pressed, hung by color, from light to dark, and spoke without turning. "I wouldn't be surprised if he left that housekeeper detailed instructions as to what to clean up in the event of his death. Judging by his will and the look of this house, he seems to have been a very organized man."

"Too organized."

He agreed. "You would almost think that nobody lived here."

"Well, Marcus. Nobody does anymore…."

He felt a flash of heat under his skin. Annoyance. Worse. He turned to her. "You think I should have made up with him, don't you?"

She took his hand. He had to actively stop himself from jerking away. She wrapped that hand around her waist and then took his other hand and guided it behind her, too, so that he held her in a loose embrace. After she'd arranged his hands to her satisfaction, she put her own on his shoulders. Softly, she told him, "I think you're a good man and you did what you could. I think you had a lot to forgive him for. Maybe too much."

"That's no answer." He growled the words at her.

She kept her chin tilted up, her gaze on his. "Sorry. It's the only answer I've got right now. This is all very sad. He did well for himself in America, but it looks like he was all alone."

"And whose fault was that?"

"Marcus. Does it really have to be someone's fault?"

He was the one who looked away. "There's a safe in the study." He took her hands from his shoulders and stepped back from her. Grabbing the list he'd set on the table, he turned for the door to the hallway.

The study had cherrywood wainscoting to waist height. He pressed a panel. It swung wide. The safe was behind it. He went on one knee to enter the combination. It opened.

Inside there was a small stack of cash on top of a large yellow envelope. He counted the money. Two thousand dollars in hundreds. He supposed it belonged to him now— like everything else in this too-orderly, too-quiet house. But for some reason, he couldn't bear to take it. So he set it aside and picked up the envelope.

"What is it?" Rhia had followed him. She hovered in the doorway to the hall.

He rose, carried the envelope to the desk and poured out the contents.

Disappointment tightened the skin on the back of his

neck and made a hard ball packed with nothing in the pit of his stomach. "Just another copy of the damn will."

She came to stand at his shoulder and asked in a low and careful voice, "What is it you're looking for?"

He sank into the desk chair. "I don't know. Something more than this. Letters. Photographs. Something… personal. Something *real*."

She put her hand on his shoulder. "I think we should look through the house, open all the drawers, go through everything. See what we can find."

He reached up and clasped her fingers. They felt good in his. They felt right. Funny how just the touch of her hand did so much to make the emptiness bearable. He shouldn't be so gruff with her. But somehow, gruff was the only way he could be right then. "Doesn't that seem a little disrespectful, going through Roland's drawers and closets when I never even knew the man?"

She moved in closer, wrapped her arms around his neck and bent close to him. He breathed in the faint scent of jasmine and the knot of nothing in his gut eased a little more. She whispered, "What I think is that you need more than an empty house, a pile of money and another copy of your father's will. And I think we are going to keep looking until we find what you need."

Beneath the orderly rows of matched, perfectly rolled socks in Roland's sock drawer, Marcus found two pictures. In one, a pretty, very serious-looking woman wearing dark trousers, a black vest, a white shirt and a bow tie stood by the world-famous Fountain of the Three Sirens in front of Casino d'Ambre. On the back of that snapshot was one word: Isa.

The other picture was of Roland and the same woman. They sat at a table in an outdoor café. His arm was across her shoulders, an open bottle of wine and two half-full wineglasses in front of them. Roland was grinning at her. Isa was smiling back at him. It was a joyous, open smile with just a hint of mischief in it.

He called Rhia in from the other room and showed her what he'd found.

She clapped her hands at the sight. "Personal pictures. Oh, I'm so glad. I knew we'd find *something*." She read his mother's name on the back of the one by the fountain, then turned it over to study the image on the front. "Oh, Marcus. She looks so…subdued. It's hard to tell much about her from this one."

"The other one's better, I think."

She took the second one and stared at it for a long time. "This is the good one. She looks like she doesn't want to be anywhere else but right there, at that table, with that man. He looks like he feels the same about her. As though they have it all, don't you think?"

He wasn't willing to go that far. "They look as though they're having a good time. I'll say that much."

"Well, *I* would guess from this picture that they were happy together, at least for a while…."

What did it matter? They would never really know. "All right. Let's think of it that way. Once, they were happy."

"Yes. I like that. I truly do." She gave him back the photo and left him to return to the search.

It was only a few minutes later that she called him into the study and showed him a four-drawer file cabinet in the closet. The bottom drawer was labeled "Marcus." It contained a series of reports and a large number of photographs compiled by the investigators Roland had hired to gather information about the son he'd abandoned. The first report was fifteen years old.

"It fits," Rhia said, excitement vibrating in her voice.

"He came to America, spent several years building his business. But he never forgot you. When he had some money, he started trying to find out what had happened to you."

He wasn't impressed. "Too little, too late, as far as I'm concerned." The more he thought about it, the more he realized he didn't need to know any more about the long-dead past.

She was giving him a look that seemed to speak volumes, but she didn't say anything.

That look got under his skin. "He abandoned both my mother and me. In the end, that's all that really matters to me."

She did speak up then. "And he spent his life paying for that one terrible decision."

"I would say he did all right for himself."

"Marcus, he was alone. He never married, never had a family."

"Because he threw away his family. And what do you mean, *one* terrible decision? I would say that there were at least two of those. He didn't call for help when he found my mother's body. And then he took me, only to abandon me."

"Because he was afraid. He didn't know what would happen if he called for help. I can see that he might have thought he would be blamed for her death."

"Why would he even think he would be blamed if it wasn't in some way true? And now I say it all out loud I'm seeing that it's more than two bad decisions. There was a whole ugly string of them. And that's if we can even believe his story that she was dead when he got there."

"Marcus. Come on. I'm sure that he wouldn't have—"

He shoved the file drawer shut. It slammed hard against the frame. "I'm finished here. None of this stuff means a damn thing to me."

She wouldn't give it up. "My mother always says that forgiveness is everything, that when we forgive, we free *ourselves* more than the one who needs our forgiveness."

"Heard that before," he told her flatly. "Raised by nuns, remember?"

"I'm only saying that the more you learn about who Roland and Isa were, about what really happened between them, the more you'll begin to see that they did the best they could."

He took her arm and pulled her out of that closet. "Enough."

"But, Marcus…"

He didn't need to know any more about his mother and Roland and their tragic love—or whatever it was between them that had ended with his mother dying all alone and him abandoned on a cold cathedral step. It was over and done. Isa and Roland were gone. Beyond suffering. Beyond retribution for their sins.

Whatever their sins might actually have been.

What mattered was now. This moment. What mattered was this fine, true-hearted, beautiful woman before him. His child that she carried inside of her body. What mattered was this chance he had with her.

Against all odds. In spite of everything—his own blind, foolish pride most of all.

"Marcus, have you heard a word that I've said?"

"Every word, Rhia."

"I only think that it could help you, to know more about them."

He reminded her, gently now, "You said that already."

"But I'm trying to—"

"Shh. No more." He put his finger under her chin, tipped her soft mouth up—and claimed it.

She stiffened at first. And then a choked little sigh escaped her. And then she slid her hands up over his chest and clasped them behind his neck. She melted into him.

He tasted her sweetness and knew that, no matter what happened, no matter if she refused to marry him every time he asked for the rest of their lives, he would never leave her. He would be there, for her. And for the child. He would never be a man who walked away from the ones who mattered most of all.

They left that house soon after. He took the two pictures from the sock drawer with him and the list of codes and the ring of keys. Everything else, he left behind.

He told the driver to take them to their favorite burger stand. And then they went to a movie—a comedy—at Mann's Chinese Theater.

That evening, they stood out on the balcony at the Beverly Wilshire and he told her that, no, he didn't want to go to Roland's cabin in the Sierras. "What I want is to call Anthony Evans and find out if there's anything else I need to do to settle my father's estate. And then I want to call the Neptune Society and ask them to ship Roland's ashes to me. And as soon as all that's done, I want to go home."

She caught her lower lip between her pretty white teeth. "I know I should just let it be...."

Her hair was up. He wanted it down, wanted to sift the strands between his fingers. So he started pulling out pins, letting them fall where they might. One pinged against the railing. And another after that.

She didn't object—not to his taking her hair down, anyway. "We might find more pictures, up at that cabin, learn more about your mother...."

"Forget the cabin. It doesn't matter."

"But—"

He bent close, pressed a quick, hard kiss against those

sweet red lips. "Shh." He whispered against her mouth, "I want to go home." He combed her hair with his fingers. It felt so warm and soft and silky. And then he took her by the waist. "Come here. Closer…" He slid his hands down, cupped her firm bottom and pulled her in tight to him. He was already half-hard.

And he was getting harder. He wanted her. All of her. He wanted her clothes off. He wanted that now.

"Marcus…" She sounded slightly breathless. He liked her that way. He started unbuttoning the sleeveless pink shirt she wore. She pushed at his chest. But not all that hard. "We should really…talk about…" He covered her mouth and sucked the rest of that sentence right out of her.

She tasted so good and he didn't want to talk anymore.

He was through talking for one day. More than through.

He wanted her smooth, pretty body. He wanted her ardent sighs. He wanted to kiss all her most secret places.

And then he wanted to bury himself in her sweetness for a long, satisfying ride.

He had all of her clothes off in less than a minute. He'd always been good with his hands. Her little pink shirt and her short skirt, the red thong she wore underneath. And the lacy pink bra, too.

About then, she started pushing at his shoulders again. "Marcus, I'm standing here on this balcony naked as the day I was born…."

"You still have those sandals." He tried to capture her mouth again.

"Anyone might glance up here and see me."

He scooped her high against his chest. "Then we should go inside."

She made a sound that might have been a protest, but then she wrapped her arms around his neck and tucked her head against his shoulder. He carried her in and set her down in front of a fat wing chair. She blinked up at him, bewildered. "What are you *doing?*"

"Here. Let me show you." He took her velvety shoulders and pushed her gently down into the chair.

"Marcus..."

"It's fine." He knelt before her and eased her shapely knees wide. "Just keep saying my name."

"Oh! Marcus..."

"That's the way." He bent close, nuzzled the soft dark curls that covered her where she was hot and wet already—and open for him.

She said his name more insistently and breathlessly, too, as he kissed her. He started with quick, teasing kisses. And then he made those kisses longer. Deeper. He used his tongue and his fingers, too.

In no time, she reached for him. She kicked off her sandals and braced her feet up on the arms of the chair. She held his head tight and close. He breathed in heat and vanilla and jasmine and musk, tasting her in that most intimate way as he kissed her, coaxing her, driving her steadily to the brink.

And over.

She held him tighter than ever then. He could hardly breathe and he didn't care. The slick, hot center of her pulsed against his mouth. He drank her in as she cried his name out good and loud. When she sagged back to the chair cushion, he gathered her limp body into his arms again and carried her to the bedroom, where he set her so carefully onto the turned-back bed.

He got rid of his clothes. She reached for him as he came down to her. He buried himself in her glorious wet heat and forgot everything but the feel of her beneath him, the miracle of her flawless skin under his hands.

They made it last. By the time she went over the edge,

taking him with her, he was lost to all but the wonder of her body locked to his.

Afterward, he held her. He stroked her hair and ran his hands down the sweet, tender bumps of her spine. She fell asleep and so did he.

In the middle of the night he woke. She lay against him, smooth and tempting, smelling of sex and flowers. He drew her even closer and made love to her all over again.

By the time they returned to Montedoro on Wednesday, Rhia had resigned herself to the fact that Marcus was not going to try and find out any more about his lost father—or about his mother who had died so tragically on the night of his birth.

Yes, she felt it would be better for him to know more, to find out everything he could. But he'd been through so much in his life. Too much. If he'd had enough, who was she to tell him he had to find out more?

In the end, although she could try and get him to see the wisdom of making real and lasting peace with his past, she couldn't do it for him. If he said he was satisfied with the way things stood now, it was her job to accept his decision.

Acceptance was part of loving.

And Rhia did love. She loved Marcus. She knew that now.

Maybe she had always loved him. Or maybe, since Montana, she'd learned to love him again. She didn't know for sure which. And it didn't really matter. What mattered was that at some point during their second time together in Southern California, she had come to grips with the fact that she loved him *now*.

She loved his bravery and his goodness, loved his unflagging determination to do the right thing. She loved that he wanted so fervently to be a good father. She loved how, though he'd started with less than nothing, he'd manage to create a meaningful, productive life for himself. She loved how hard he was trying to tell her about himself, to share with her all the secrets he would never tell another.

She loved the way he laughed—just a little unwillingly, as though someone might catch him at it and steal the moment of humor away. She loved his intelligence and his wonderful, powerful body.

She loved *him*. It was that enormous and that simple. And she understood now that it was very likely she always would love him.

For her, the decision was made at last. She wanted to make a life with him. To be his wife as well as his devoted lover and the mother of their coming child. She was ready to say yes as soon as he asked her to marry him again.

Unfortunately, though he continued to stay with her at the villa and to treat her with tenderness, consideration, passion and what seemed like deep affection, he never actually said that he loved her. And a month after they returned to Montedoro from Los Angeles, he had yet to mention marriage again.

## Chapter Fourteen

"It's so simple," Allie said.

Rhia braced herself for a lecture.

It was a little past noon on the second Wednesday in August and they were sharing lunch at Allie's villa, which was smaller than Rhia's, not in the harbor area and without nearly as nice a view. But it was closer to the palace and the stables where Allie spent most of her time, so she was perfectly happy living there.

What Allie was *not* happy with was Rhia and the way she was handling this problem with Marcus. She scolded, "You have to tell him that you love him. And then you have to say that you do want to marry him, that you've made up your mind at last."

Rhia picked up her water glass, but plunked it back down without taking a sip. "You don't understand."

"Oh, yes, I do. *You're* the one who's making this way too complicated and impossibly difficult."

"No. No, I'm not."

Allie ate a scallop and then stuck her fork in her linguine and twirled up a nice big mouthful. "Yes, you most definitely are. You know what the Americans say."

"Please don't tell me."

"No guts, no glory."

"Didn't I ask you not to tell me?"

Allie ate her fat forkful of linguine with obvious relish. "You're the one who went on and on about how you would never marry a man just because you were having his baby. Well, now you don't have that problem anymore. You *want* to marry Marcus because you realize he's the man for you. So do it. Tell the man you love him and can't wait to spend your life with him."

"But what if he's changed his mind?" Rhia's stomach churned. She pushed her plate away. This conversation did not lend itself to the enjoyment of scallops, even if they were fresh-caught and perfectly prepared. She put her hand on her stomach, which was growing rounder by the day. She had a definite baby bump now. Yesterday, at the museum, as they ticked off their progress with the final preparations for the Adele Canterone exhibit in two weeks, she'd caught Claudine eyeing her belly. Rhia was certain that the museum director had guessed she was pregnant— not that it really mattered that Claudine had guessed. After all, it wouldn't be long now before everyone would know.

Everyone including the paparazzi. Rhia knew how such things went. She would be all over the tabloids, seen from the side, her bump prominently displayed for the whole world to ogle and gossip about. She could picture the headlines now: *Bodyguard's Love Child. Princess Rhia's Baby Bump. A Baby But No Wedding Bells for Princess Rhia.*

Ugh.

All right, yes. She had known this would happen. She

had told herself that she was prepared for it, that she would get through all the unpleasantness of being just scandalous enough to get the attention of the tabloids even if she was only a far-down-the-birth-order princess in a family full of potential heirs.

And she *was* prepared.

But now that she knew she loved Marcus and wanted to marry him, it didn't have to be all that bad. If they got married, the scandal would quickly fade away.

But they *couldn't* get married.

Because Marcus hadn't asked her and she was too afraid to ask him.

Allie was not through lecturing. "What are you worried about? He's not going to change his mind about marrying you. I mean, please. How many times has he asked you already?"

"Um. Seven? Nine? I'm not sure."

"Well, and there's another reason why you should do the asking."

"What are you talking about now?"

"Rhia. It's your *turn.*"

"My *turn?* There are no *turns* when it comes to proposing marriage."

"In your case, there ought to be."

Rhia pushed her plate a little farther away. "All right. I admit that I really *should* just go ahead and ask him."

"You admit the simple truth. Will wonders never cease?"

"But I *can't.*"

Allie gave her a look of pitiless disapproval. "Oh, yes, you can. You're not a wimp. Stop acting like one."

"You don't understand."

"You're right. I don't."

"Allie…" Her voice failed her. Her throat had clutched

and her eyes burned with hot tears. "What if he turns me down?" There. She had said it.

And Allie was not impressed. "He's not going to turn you down. Even if he wasn't crazy in love with you—which it's obvious to everyone but you that he is—he wants to be married to you because of the baby."

"How many times do I have to explain that I do not want a husband who only wants me because of the baby? And besides, he's...different lately. He's more relaxed. Happier."

Allie threw up her hands. "You're making my arguments for me. He is different. He's a happy man now. I know that he'll say yes. Just do it. Just ask him."

"But what if he says no?"

"Then you'll still have turned him down six—or eight—times more than he did you."

"Five or seven," she corrected in a tiny little voice that was cracking around the edges.

Allie blinked. "Huh?"

"Allie, I begged him."

"Wait. What? I thought you hadn't even said 'I love you' yet."

"But I did."

"When?"

"Six years ago." A rough, ugly sob escaped her. "I stood in the dirt in front of a run-down farmhouse in the South of France, and I pleaded with him to give our relationship a chance. I cried right there in front of him, like a pathetic, hopeless fool with no pride whatsoever and I told him that I loved him. And he said it was over and he wasn't interested and would I please just go away."

"Oh." Allie gulped. "That."

"Yes. That."

"I guess I had kind of put all that old awfulness right out of my mind."

"Well, I haven't. And I…I can't do that again." The tears overflowed then. She couldn't stop them. They rolled down her cheeks and her nose started running. She tried to swipe the flood away with the back of her hand.

Allie gave up all pretense of talking tough. "Oh, my darling. I'm sorry. I shouldn't have jumped all over you. I'm an ass. Don't…" She got up, grabbed a handful of tissues, scooted to Rhia's side and gave them to her. Then she bent to wrap her arms around her. "Dearest. You mustn't."

"I can't help it." Rhia tried to mop up the flood a little, but the tears just kept coming. "I want to tell him, but I can't do it. I just…I can't, that's all."

"Well, all right. All right, then." Allie patted her hair, stroked her back. "You go ahead. You just cry it out…"

"Oh, Allie, you're right. You are. I am being so very, very stupid over this."

Allie had totally surrendered her tough-love approach. She said what a good sister should say. "My darling, you are not in any way stupid."

"Yes, I am! Stupid, dumb and way too emotional. It's the hormones. Or at least that's what I keep telling myself…." She broke down and sobbed some more.

Allie held her and tenderly stroked her hair. "Whatever it is, it doesn't matter. Sometimes a woman just needs a good cry."

So Rhia cried. And Allie went on holding her, whispering that it would be all right.

When the tears finally stopped, Rhia blew her nose and wiped her eyes and retired to the powder room to try and repair the ravages before returning to the museum.

As she was leaving, Allie couldn't resist getting in the last word. "Just tell him you love him. If you could only do that much…"

That evening when she got home, Marcus was waiting.

He had a big bouquet of fire lilies for her and a bright-purple bruise high on his cheekbone.

The flowers cheered her up. A man who didn't want to marry her wouldn't be bringing her flowers.

Would he?

She thanked him with a kiss, gave Yvonne the flowers to put in a vase and took Marcus to the kitchen where she found a bag of peas in the freezer and made him hold it to the side of his face.

He told her he'd trained that morning with Denis and then with Rene.

"You fought with them, you mean." She tried not to sound disapproving and knew that she probably failed.

He didn't deny it. "That Denis has a deadly right hook." He said it with what could only be called admiration. "He's not a bad guy, really. Neither is Rene…"

He was coming to *accept* his childhood enemies? Would wonders never cease?

She said, only a little bit smugly, "Do you realize you are sounding almost forgiving?"

He shrugged. "Won't the sisters at St. Stephen's be proud?" And then he told her the important news. He'd had a meeting with her brother Alexander and Sir Hector Anteros that afternoon. "My days providing security to the princely family are numbered. I'm being promoted to commandant and over the next few years I will be groomed for the leadership of the CCU."

"Alex is stepping down?"

"He says he will be spending more time with Lili and their twins in Alagonia and focusing more on his duties there. He is the father of the future king, after all."

It really was exciting news. "Oh, Marcus. Congratulations. How wonderful."

"Yes, it is, isn't it?" He was so confident, so self-assured, standing there in the kitchen with a bag of frozen peas against his handsome face. "I'm the man for that post and it's satisfying that I'll have it." His eyes sparked with wry humor. "Even if I do have something of an unfair advantage...."

She frowned up at him. "What advantage?"

He reached out, caught a lock of her air and tugged on it. "Well, Rhia. You."

She tried to read his thoughts in his expression, and failed utterly. So she asked, "Does it bother you that your relationship with me would make my brother more likely to choose you as his successor?"

He chuckled then. It was a real chuckle—good-natured, lighthearted. "It might if I didn't know that I fully deserve this promotion and will give it my all."

"So then, it doesn't bother you?"

"Not in the least."

Rhia tried not to gape at him, not to demand to know what he'd done with the real Marcus. He'd always been so proud. Too proud. And she'd dreamed that he might somehow become a little more relaxed about things. That he might see his own value and simply accept the good things that came his way. Like for instance, that a princess might have fallen in love with him all those years ago.

Apparently, he had finally learned to do just that—at least when it came to his military career.

What else had changed about him? Had he come around to her original way of thinking about the baby, too? Had he come to agree that they didn't need to be married for him to be a hands-on, loving father?

He must have sensed her distress. He took the peas away from his cheek and set them on the counter. "Rhia, are you all right?"

*I love you and I want to marry you. I want that so much.*

*It's making me crazy how much I want that.* "Ahem. I, well, I have been feeling a little bit weepy today." *And I am a complete coward lately. I seem to have no idea how to say what I want.*

He reached out and laid his big hand on her rounded belly. "You're all right, though? Both of you?"

She bit her lip and nodded.

And he took her hand and led her out of the kitchen and into the bedroom they'd been sharing for almost two months now.

He took off her clothes and pushed her down to the bed, where he rubbed her feet and then massaged her back. He told her she was beautiful, even though she knew that she looked haggard and that her eyes were still red and swollen from her crying jag at Allie's. He put his big hands on her belly and he talked to the baby. He'd been doing that for a couple of weeks now, talking so softly and soothingly, saying the sweetest things.

Dear Lord. He was turning out to be an absolutely wonderful man.

If only he loved her. If only he wanted to marry her not only for the baby, but for her sake, as well. If only it could all *not* turn out the way it had six years ago.

When he finished his conversation with the baby, he kissed his way up over her belly and her breasts. He brushed a warm, soft row of kisses over her throat and her chin to her mouth. She opened for him, sighing. He kissed her some more. He kissed her everywhere. He made beautiful love to her. At the end, she almost forgot her fears enough to shout out her love for him as her climax rolled through her.

But she didn't. She held it in.

And in the morning when she woke, he was already gone for his predawn workout at the CCU training yard.

He called her at the museum later that morning. "Did I tell you that Roland's ashes arrived?"

"That's a relief." It was a complicated process, shipping cremated remains internationally.

"They came yesterday afternoon before you got home." *Home*. He had called the villa *home*. That was a good sign, wasn't it? "I got all wrapped up in telling you about my promotion and forgot to say that they were here."

"Well, I'm glad they arrived safely."

"Yes." His voice sounded far away, suddenly. "I've reserved a motorboat. I was thinking I would take care of them this afternoon."

*He* would take care of them. So, then. He wanted to do the job alone. She could accept that, could understand that it was something he might want to do without company. Still, disappointment settled on her shoulders, heavy as a cape made of lead. She yearned to be the one he needed with him at a time like this. Then he asked, "Will you meet me at four? Can you get away?" He named a slip at the pier not all that far from the villa, down in the area where the smaller boats were docked.

He wanted her to go with him! The cape of lead lifted. She felt light as air. "Yes. Of course I'll be there."

She considered going home and changing into something more casual to go out on a small boat. But then, really, this was the only sendoff the mysterious Roland was going to get. So she wore what she'd worn to work: a lightweight, fitted sheath of raw silk and a contrasting raw-silk jacket. She had a scarf in her bag in case the wind came up.

He was waiting when she got there, looking so handsome in the white uniform he'd worn the day she told him that there would be a baby. The bruise on his cheekbone from the bout with Denis was already fading. He helped her into the boat, which was larger than she'd expected, with a small cabin and a roomy cockpit.

She took a seat. The wind tugged at her hair, so she put on her scarf as he dealt with the mooring lines. When he took the wheel, she asked him, "The ashes?"

"In the cabin." He put on his aviator sunglasses, started the engine and backed the boat from the slip.

They were quiet with each other as he eased the boat through the obstacles in the crowded harbor. It wasn't long before they passed between the twin points at harbor's end and into the open sea.

He turned the boat and followed the coastline south for a time. She watched the glorious, gray-green hills of her country moving by, the red roofs of villas so inviting through the lush canopy of trees. The Prince's Palace, home of her childhood, appeared on its high, craggy promontory, growing larger as they came even with it. The sun was warm on her shoulders, but the wind had a bite to it. Seagulls soared on the air currents overhead. She could hear their distant calls.

Finally, he said, "I think it's safe to drift for a little." He left the wheel, ducked below and emerged with a plain black box.

He took off his sunglasses, put on his hat and took the box to the landward side, where the wind was at his back. Then he turned to her. She remained in the seat by the wheel, unsure of what her involvement should be. He tucked the box under one arm, and held out his free hand to her.

She had that light-as-air feeling again as she rose and moved to his side.

He caught her hand, brought to his lips. "I know you're going to want to say a few words…."

She gave him a wobbly little smile. "Yes. Please."

They turned together toward the coast. He opened the box.

The wind pushed at her back. He folded down the plastic lining and tipped the box so the ashes drifted out slowly. She started the Lord's Prayer. When she finished that, she recited the Twenty-Third Psalm, all while he carefully shook free the grainy gray powder studded with white bits that had to be bone. Some of the powder made a film on the surface of the blue water, some the wind carried away toward the shore.

When it was finally done, he took the box below. Then he put his sunglasses back on and went to the helm once more. She reclaimed her seat beside him. He started up the boat and drove them back the way they had come.

It was all strangely dreamlike, she thought. Dreamlike and so peaceful.

They reentered the harbor. He maneuvered the boat back to the slip, eased it cleanly into place and tied it down again. He took her hand and helped her back onto the pier.

"Let's walk a little," he said, and tucked her fingers around his arm. He led her to the Promenade and they strolled along it for a time. There was a man with a camera back on the pier, snapping pictures of them. And another man, also armed with a camera, who seemed to keep popping up in her side vision as they walked.

She didn't care. She tuned them out. Marcus didn't seem to mind, either.

People called to her and waved. She smiled at them, returning their greetings. Eventually, they came to that same bench beneath the tree where they'd sat together on that first night he moved into her villa.

"This looks familiar," he said. They sat side by side in the shade. He took off his hat and his sunglasses and turned to her. "It meant a lot to me, that you were with me."

"To me, too."

"I think it was...nice." He touched the side of her face. She smiled into his eyes as he untied her scarf. "Peaceful." She made a sound of agreement as he pulled the scarf away. He gave it to her and then began removing the pins from her hair.

That made her smile. "You do know that we are probably being photographed."

"I don't care. You're here with me. That's what matters. Give me your hand." She did. He put the pins in it, on top of the scarf. She wadded the whole thing up and stuck it in her bag as he combed her hair with his fingers. "There."

She gazed into his almost-green eyes and felt tears welling in hers. "Oh, Marcus...."

He touched her cheek, wiped a tear away with his thumb. "Don't cry. I love you, Rhiannon. I've always loved you."

She blinked in amazement. The miracle had happened, just like that. He'd said the words she needed so much to hear, said them so she knew he meant them. At last. She sniffed, shut her eyes, willed the tears down. Because she knew then. She knew...everything. "Oh, Marcus..."

He gazed at her so earnestly. "You made me tell you about that other woman, the one I never actually met. But that was only a sad little story I told myself, a pitiful consolation for the hard fact that I couldn't let myself have you. You were always the only one. Always. Please believe me."

"How could I not?" she whispered. "It's been the same for me."

"I know I hurt you."

She let it out then. The old, awful, brutal truth. "I begged you to give us another chance. While you just stood there on the steps of that empty house and looked at me like you only wanted me to stop. I *pleaded* with you, threw my poor heart at your feet. Still, you sent me away."

"I was wrong."

"You were. Terribly wrong. I so longed to hate you for that."

"Say that you didn't."

"No. I wanted to. I couldn't. I could never hate you, not really. I love you. More than anything. I will never, ever stop loving you, Marcus."

He took her hand again. "I've been waiting. Trying to show you that I can be the man you need for a lifetime. That we can be together in every way. Stand together. Love together. Be the ones who make the future. Raise our baby together."

"Oh, God." Tears scalded the back of her throat again. She swallowed them down and made herself come clean. "I thought...that maybe you had changed your mind."

"No. Never. I've been an idiot, but not anymore."

"Oh, Marcus...."

"Marry me, Rhia. Be my wife."

She looked down and he was slipping a diamond onto her finger. "Oh! Oh, it's beautiful."

"Just say yes. Tell me yes."

And she did. "Yes," she said clearly and firmly. "Forever and for always, Marcus. That's how I want it to be."

And he grabbed her close and kissed her long and slow and deep, right there on the Promenade for all the world to see.

## Epilogue

The pictures of the bodyguard's proposal on the Promenade at Colline d'Ambre appeared in various tabloids worldwide three days later.

Noah Cordell saw them. Not because he was a big fan of the stuff they printed in the scandal sheets, but because Noah made it his business to keep up with everything that happened in the Bravo-Calabretti family.

Noah dreamed big. They called him brash and bold. Difficult to know, yet charming with a boyish quality that had helped him to get ahead.

He had started out on the mean streets of Los Angeles with nothing. At the age of eighteen, he'd enrolled in business school at night and gone to work days as a laborer for a guy who flipped houses—and loved horses. Within two years, Noah was flipping houses himself. And getting invited to his new boss's ranch, where he quickly learned to love horses, too. Noah moved up and he moved up fast.

By the end of his real estate career, Noah was building office towers in all the major real estate markets. But then, with his unerring feel for the markets, he sensed the crash was coming. He got out just in time, and he took his fortune with him. Since then, he'd been living the good life, looking after his investments, watching his money grow.

Noah thoroughly enjoyed the fruits of his ambition and labor. Five years ago, as a thirtieth birthday present to himself, he'd bought a sprawling, luxurious horse ranch in Santa Barbara. He'd moved in, bringing his frail younger sister, and the housekeeper who'd once been his sister's foster mom. More recently, while pursuing his interest in fast, expensive cars and beautiful women, he'd wrangled an introduction to Prince Damien of Montedoro. Noah and Damien found they had a lot in common. The connection to Damien was a big step in the right direction. Noah now had a friend in the Bravo-Calabretti family.

He wanted two things from the Bravo-Calabrettis.

One, the princely family bred and trained Akhal-Teke horses. The tough, ancient, hot-blooded breed from the deserts of Turkmenistan fascinated Noah. He wanted an Akhal-Teke stallion from the palace stables of Montedoro and he intended to have one.

Two, Noah had decided it was time he got to work on his dynasty. To start a dynasty, a man needed the right woman. Noah thought that a princess would do very nicely.

But not any weird, inbred, frail kind of princess. Noah wanted a woman with guts and brains and a sense of humor. Oh, and with a family history of fertility. After all, a dynasty is predicated on the production of heirs.

It was a tall order. But Noah knew where to look to fill it. The Bravo-Calabrettis were a large, loving family. There were five sisters in that family. One of them loved horses as much as Noah did and was closely involved with the breeding and training of the Akhal-Tekes he coveted.

So Noah had concentrated on the horsey one, on finding out more about her. He'd learned that not only was she a genius with horses, she had something of a wild streak. She liked riding fast motorcycles and dancing all night in working-class bars.

There were a lot of pictures of her on the internet. Noah had studied them at length. She had brown hair and dimples, eyes that sometimes looked gray and sometimes blue and sometimes a strange, haunting color in between. Her smile dazzled.

Yeah. She was the one, all right. Her Serene Highness Alice would definitely do.

* * * * *

*Watch for Alice and Noah's story,*
*HOW TO MARRY A PRINCESS,*
*coming in November 2013,*
*only from Harlequin Special Edition.*

## COMING NEXT MONTH
## from Harlequin® Special Edition®
### AVAILABLE APRIL 23, 2013

#### #2257 A WEAVER VOW
*Return to the Double C*
**Allison Leigh**
When Erik Clay makes a commitment, it is forever, and when he meets Isabella Lockhart, he knows forever is what he wants. Unfortunately, there's an eleven-year-old boy whose heart is just as bruised as Isabella's standing squarely in their way....

#### #2258 EXPECTING FORTUNE'S HEIR
*The Fortunes of Texas: Southern Invasion*
**Cindy Kirk**
Shane Fortune is accustomed to women using his family for money, so when the cute and spunky Lia Serrano tells him that she is pregnant with his baby after a one-night stand, he is seriously skeptical. But after spending more time together, he can't help but hope the baby is truly his....

#### #2259 MADE IN TEXAS!
*Byrds of a Feather*
**Crystal Green**
After inheriting a share of property, independent woman Donna Byrd came to Texas to build a B&B. She'd help market the inn then head right back to her city life...at least, that was the plan until she met cowboy Caleb Granger!

#### #2260 A DADDY FOR DILLON
*Men of the West*
**Stella Bagwell**
Ranch foreman Laramie Jones's life is all work and no play, until Leyla Chee arrives as the ranch's new chef with her young son in tow. It's true that Laramie has won little Dillon's admiration, but can he charm the protective mommy, too?

#### #2261 THE TEXAN'S SURPRISE BABY
**Gina Wilkins**
After a passionate one-night stand with dashing Texas P.I. Andrew Walker, the commitment-shy Hannah Bell refuses to see the relationship go any further. Six months later, their paths cross again, but this time he has a surprisingly special reason to win Hannah's heart....

#### #2262 FATHER BY CHOICE
**Amanda Berry**
On the verge of a promotion, workaholic Brady Ward learns that he has a seven-year-old daughter living with her mother—his ex, Maggie!—in a small town. Can the big-city businessman ditch the climb up the corporate ladder for a simpler life with the family he never knew he had?

You can find more information on upcoming Harlequin® titles, free excerpts and more at www.Harlequin.com.

HSECNM0413

# REQUEST YOUR FREE BOOKS!

## 2 FREE NOVELS PLUS 2 FREE GIFTS!

### ♦HARLEQUIN®

# SPECIAL EDITION

## Life, Love & Family

**YES!** Please send me 2 FREE Harlequin® Special Edition novels and my 2 FREE gifts (gifts are worth about $10). After receiving them, if I don't wish to receive any more books, I can return the shipping statement marked "cancel." If I don't cancel, I will receive 6 brand-new novels every month and be billed just $4.49 per book in the U.S. or $5.24 per book in Canada. That's a savings of at least 14% off the cover price! It's quite a bargain! Shipping and handling is just 50¢ per book in the U.S. and 75¢ per book in Canada.* I understand that accepting the 2 free books and gifts places me under no obligation to buy anything. I can always return a shipment and cancel at any time. Even if I never buy another book, the two free books and gifts are mine to keep forever.

235/335 HDN FVTV

Name                                    (PLEASE PRINT)

Address                                                                          Apt. #

City                                    State/Prov.                    Zip/Postal Code

Signature (if under 18, a parent or guardian must sign)

Mail to the **Harlequin® Reader Service:**
**IN U.S.A.:** P.O. Box 1867, Buffalo, NY 14240-1867
**IN CANADA:** P.O. Box 609, Fort Erie, Ontario L2A 5X3

**Want to try two free books from another line?**
**Call 1-800-873-8635 or visit www.ReaderService.com.**

* Terms and prices subject to change without notice. Prices do not include applicable taxes. Sales tax applicable in N.Y. Canadian residents will be charged applicable taxes. Offer not valid in Quebec. This offer is limited to one order per household. Not valid for current subscribers to Harlequin Special Edition books. All orders subject to credit approval. Credit or debit balances in a customer's account(s) may be offset by any other outstanding balance owed by or to the customer. Please allow 4 to 6 weeks for delivery. Offer available while quantities last.

**Your Privacy**—The Harlequin® Reader Service is committed to protecting your privacy. Our Privacy Policy is available online at www.ReaderService.com or upon request from the Harlequin Reader Service.

We make a portion of our mailing list available to reputable third parties that offer products we believe may interest you. If you prefer that we not exchange your name with third parties, or if you wish to clarify or modify your communication preferences, please visit us at www.ReaderService.com/consumerschoice or write to us at Harlequin Reader Service Preference Service, P.O. Box 9062, Buffalo, NY 14269. Include your complete name and address.

HSEI3

SPECIAL EXCERPT FROM

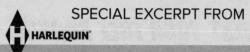

**H** HARLEQUIN®

SPECIAL EDITION

USA TODAY *bestselling author Allison Leigh*
*brings us a sneak peek of A WEAVER VOW,*
*a new tale of love, loss and second chances in her*
RETURN TO THE DOUBLE-C *miniseries for*
*Harlequin® Special Edition®.*

\*\*\*

*Murphy, please don't get into more trouble.*

Whatever had made her think she could be a better parent to Murphy than his other options? He needed a man around, not just a woman he could barely tolerate.

He needed his father.

And now all they had was each other.

Isabella Lockhart couldn't bear to think about it.

"It was an accident!" Murphy yelled. "Dude! That's my bat. You can't just take my bat!"

"I just did, *dude*," the man returned flatly. He closed his hand over Murphy's thin shoulder and forcibly moved him away from Isabella.

Isabella rounded on the man, gaping at him. He was wearing a faded brown ball cap and aviator sunglasses that hid his eyes. "Take your hand off him! Who do you think you are?"

"The man your boy decided to aim at with his blasted baseball." His jaw was sharp and shadowed by brown stubble and his lips were thinned.

"I did not!" Murphy screamed right into Isabella's ear.

She winced, then pointed. "Go sit down."

She drew in a calming breath and turned her head into the breeze that she'd begun to suspect never died here in Weaver, Wyoming, before facing the man again. "I'm Isabella Lockhart," she began.

"I know who you are."

She'd been in Weaver only a few weeks, but it really was a small town if people she'd never met already knew who she was.

"I'm sure we can resolve whatever's happened here, Mr. uh—?"

"Erik Clay."

Focusing on the woman in front of him was a lot safer than focusing on the skinny black-haired hellion sprawled on Ruby's bench.

She tucked her white-blond hair behind her ear with a visibly shaking hand. Bleached blond, he figured, considering the eyes that she turned toward the back of his truck were such a dark brown they were nearly black.

Even angry as he was, he wasn't blind to the whole effect. Weaver's newcomer was a serious looker.

\*\*\*

*Don't miss A WEAVER VOW*
*by* USA TODAY *bestselling author Allison Leigh.*

*Available in May 2013 from*
*Harlequin® Special Edition® wherever books are sold.*

Copyright © 2013 by Allison Leigh.

HSEEXPO413

## SPECIAL EDITION

### Life, Love and Family

*EXPECTING FORTUNE'S HEIR*
by Cindy Kirk

Shane Fortune is accustomed to women using his
family for money, so when the cute and spunky
Lia Serrano tells him that she is pregnant with his
baby after a one-night stand, he is seriously skeptical.
But after spending more time together, he can't help
but hope the baby is truly his....

## Look for the next book in
*The Fortunes of Texas:
Southern Invasion*

*Available in May from Harlequin Special Edition,
wherever books are sold.*

**⊕ HARLEQUIN®**

# SPECIAL EDITION

## Life, Love and Family

## *MADE IN TEXAS!*
by Crystal Green

After inheriting a share of property, independent
woman Donna Byrd came to Texas to build a
B and B. She'd help market the inn then head right
back to her city life...at least, that was the plan until
she met cowboy Caleb Granger!

## Look for the next story in the *Byrds of a Feather* miniseries next month.

*Available in May 2013 from Harlequin Special Edition,
wherever books are sold.*

www.Harlequin.com

HSE65741

# Love the Harlequin book you just read?

### Your opinion matters.

**Review this book on your favorite book site, review site, blog or your own social media properties and share your opinion with other readers!**

**Be sure to connect with us at:**
Harlequin.com/Newsletters
Facebook.com/HarlequinBooks
Twitter.com/HarlequinBooks

HREVIEWS